LAND OF THE SEAL PEOPLE

LAND OF THE SEAL PEOPLE

Duncan Williamson
Edited by Linda Williamson

BIRLINN

This edition first published in 2010 by
Birlinn Limited
West Newington House
10 Newington Road
Edinburgh
EH9 1QS

www.birlinn.co.uk

Copyright © Linda Williamson

First published in 1992 as *Tales of the Sea People: Scottish Folk Tales*
by Canongate, Edinburgh

ISBN 978 1 84158 880 3

British Library Cataloguing-in-Publication Data
A catalogue record for this book is available from the British Library

Typeset by Hewer Text UK Ltd, Edinburgh
Printed and bound by CPI Cox & Wyman, Reading

To Betsy Jane

Contents

Acknowledgements

We are grateful for the network of storytellers worldwide who continue to tell the supernatural tales of the sea. The devotion to Duncan Williamson and his seal stories has been the key motivation for this work. Special thanks to my mentor David Campbell; the director of the Scottish Storytelling Centre, Donald Smith; Duncan's close associates, Hugh Lupton, Helen East, Ben Haggarty, Amy Douglas and Jenny Pearson. Research and writing of *Land of the Seal People*, the traditional stories of Argyll, has been supported by a Scottish Arts Council professional development grant.

Preface

The author Duncan Williamson was born on the shores of Loch Fyne, Argyll in 1928. One of Scotland's Travelling People, and not unlike others of his ethnic minority, he is known as a storyteller of great power. *Land of the Seal People* is his collection of traditional stories from Scotland's West Country. Entertaining, scary, funny and clever; but, more importantly, these are morality tales that have taught common sense and human grace to generations of young people. As 'true' tales, they represent myths and legends kept alive in the telling and retelling by fathers to their sons – handed down through hundreds of years, from generation to generation.

The collection is a free range of stories related to seal people, who have the ability to be seals in the water but can take human form when they come on land. In seals the eyes are positioned as in our own faces; like cats and owls, they appear to share something of our nature. Williamson's 'silkie' stories, collected from Scottish travellers and country folk, magically link the two worlds, animal and human, sea and land.

The Scottish travellers called these half-seal, half-human creatures 'silkies', a word derived from the softness of a sealskin. It can forecast the weather: before a storm the hair rises up telling you it's going to be rough; when the sun comes out the sealskin lies smooth and soft and silky. And it is not surprising that many of the seal stories feature the magical properties of a long dark coat. The skin of the seal is surrendered at death for the next-generation silkie.

Not all seals are silkies, but some have the power to take over the form of a human being, be a human or take away a human to become a seal. To have the command of being one of the seal people, your mother or father must have married one of the seal-folk. A human makes love to the seal not as an animal, but as a person, a seal-woman or a seal-man. Children who are born of a human and a seal have the power to transform into either, be a human or be a seal.

But the importance of the silkie is its part in the otherworld or after-life. This is explained by the teller at the beginning of his story, 'The Silkie's Baby'. And a connection to the organized religion of the village Christian church is not an infrequent theme: see also 'Shell House', 'The Cull' and 'Seal Brother'.

Because of the spiritual element of the seal people, they naturally lend themselves to characters which inhabit other lands of the folk tale world. Fairies, talking animals and supernatural creatures, for example the 700-year-old genie or the disappearing fish with human eyes pose themselves for the storyteller's attention. Seal stories are never told to the exclusion to other types of tales. And the traveller hero, Jack, is always at the door!

Animal tales and stories of the supernatural find their place in the world of the silkie with 'Rorrie and the Stag' an old Gaelic story, supposed to have been true, about the ancient rivalry of golden eagle and red deer stag. Two animal stories for Christmas are included: 'The Dog and the Peacock' and the origin of the spruce, why the robin is sacred to the evergreen tree. Without a defined narrator as source are 'The Gamekeeper' with an obsession for killing and 'Blind Angus', the oldest of the silkie tales known to Duncan. Another 'very old tale' of primitive fishing with a hand net thrown into the sea and 'supposed to have been true' is 'The Genie and the Fisherman'.

Conservation is one of the underlying themes of the book, and the reader is made aware that humans share their environment with other animals. There is a strong, enduring balance of nature in Duncan Williamson's stories. They usually hinge on some imbalance or distortion: where a wrong, something unjust, improper or ill-fated is put right, corrected and restored. In the fable 'Rorrie and the Stag', pride leads to a fall. Liars and cheats, thieves and killers, which figure in many of the stories, are not so much punished as re-educated. Understanding is learned by action and demonstration, in 'Seal Mother' and 'The Wounded Seal'. Poverty and loss of fortune are part of a cycle which turns upward naturally in 'John Broom' and 'The Genie and the Fisherman'. Generosity of spirit and those who help the lame are blessed in the Christmas stories at the centre of the collection.

Most of the seal stories here were recorded and published in two previous books by Duncan Williamson: *Tales of the Seal People* (Canongate, 1992; Interlink, 2005) and *The Genie and the Fisherman* (Cambridge University Press, 1991). Another six were recorded in 2003, and are published here for the first time. The original set of seal stories in *The Broonie, Silkies and Fairies* (Canongate 1985; Harmony Books, 1987) appeared in *TSP*; and *Land of the Seal People* incorporates fairy stories and tales of the otherworld like the earlier *Broonie* work. What all of the storyteller's seal stories have in common is the desire to impart a belief, the story's significance and context in a living oral tradition.

Duncan Williamson has storytelling in his blood. From

the campfire gatherings of his childhood to a lifetime of travelling the back roads of Scotland's shires he has gleaned lore from people of the crofting, fishing, mining, and farming communities as well as from his own travelling people.

The tales collected here stem mostly from Williamson's early years in Argyll. Some of them were told to him by country folk, crofters from the highlands and islands; others come from his own traveller friends and aged relatives. He relates the setting: 'When I was a child I was reared by the sea. I ate everything that hopped, jumped or crawled in the sea. I loved the seals. And I spent a night on an island with them. [See 'Seal Island' below.] My father was also very fond of the seals. He used to play the bagpipes to them. He would play a tune to the seals, and they would all pop their heads out of the water, stand up straight listening. It was the greatest thing in the world to see fifteen or twenty seals gathered listening, all looking every different direction! Because seals are awful fond of music, any kind, even whistling or singing. That's what attracted traveling folk to the seals in the first place.

'The travelling people really believed in the seals. My father believed they would come at night and throw stones at you, at the camps, if you were bad to them during the day. The seals or silkies will never do you any harm, not unless you are bad to them. Then they set out to teach you a lesson. If you are good to them then all good things happen, you get what you want. Silkies are only out to protect their own families, the same as the travellers.

'But I learned most of the seal stories I know directly from working with crofters and fishermen along Loch Fyne. These people didn't frankly tell stories to just anybody. They had very guarded attitudes towards their knowledge. It was sacred information told to them by their family and they meant to keep it in their family. It was only by me partly coaxing them and by accident and my being interested that I ever opened them up tot get one seal story from them!

'Now the important thing to remember is that these stories were never *made*; they were never set to any pattern. They were just "something strange according to them that actually took place". It was family history; that's the truth.

'I have felt privileged all my life to have heard these stories from the people of my homeland. At the time I never gave it a thought that I would tell it again to audiences, or one day be a "storyteller". But even at the age of thirteen I knew that these crofters and fishermen in their sixties and older were giving me something private and special. Stories from tradition are magic because they are given to you as a present – you are let into the personal lives of your friends. You are accepted as one of the family. It is my deepest responsibility to tell the stories again to you with the love and respect for their forbears.'

Most of the seal stories were told to the author personally. 'Seal Mother' is from Aunt Rachel in Tarbert, Loch Fyne, who actually joined the seal people at the end of her life. When Duncan left home at thirteen years of age he spent time along the Hebrides, Islay and Jura, the home of his ancestors, and Tiree and Barra. His origin tale of the Hebridean cormorant is part of a West Coast silkie legend, 'Fair Maid's Tresses'. An old farmer, John MacDougall of Dunscaig in Clachan, Kintyre told Duncan the 'true story' of Iain Cameron who was lost at sea and returned to his wife a changed man wearing the long coat – made from the skins of the silkie forefathers. MacDougall was also the original teller of 'Silkie Painter', a prize winning short story by Duncan (see *Tales of the Seal People*) and 'Shell House'.

No Scottish traveller story book would be complete

without the Jack tales, and *Land of the Seal People* includes
five previously unpublished: 'The Four Winds' was told
Duncan by traveller John MacDonald, an illiterate cripple
from the 1914 war; 'Jack and his Mother's Wee Puckle Corn'
is a glorious, ribald, King of the Fairies story from Duncan's
famed Granny Bella MacDonald; an Irish navvy told Duncan
'Jack and the Golden Peats', another brilliant story of the
'little people' who were plagued by a two-headed monster
snake; Duncan's oldest brother Jock told him 'Fiddler's
Doom' when he was only young. Jack shares the space
with seal people because of his innocence, purity of heart,
supernatural courage and most of all his relationship with
his mother; see 'Gull's Eggs'. In 'Seal Man' Jack's rescue of
an injured young man on the shore inspires him to believe
in the seal people.

These tales were heard by Duncan Williamson from
fishermen, crofters and others, up and down the West Coast.
Maurice Fleming of *The Scots Magazine* (December 1992)
wrote: 'They are superbly handled, as you would expect
from this acknowledged master of storytelling. I challenge
you to read them and not to feel a shade uneasy next time a
dark stranger approaches you on the beach or a seal's head
pops out of the water.'

The Silkie's Baby

In my travels many people have asked me who are the seal people, who are the silkie folk? You may ask yourself the same question. You could ask, who is God? If you live on an island and your only source of income is the sea, you depend on the sea for a livelihood for food for your family, food for your children and clothes for your children; the money you get comes from the sea – the fishes have to die so that you might survive.

But the sea is a dangerous place for people and it's a terrible thought when you lose someone you love dearly, for some people who are lost at sea are never found. And I always explain this to people on my travels in storytelling so they have a little idea. But if you're brought up with the culture of the sea and the sea folk and the fishermen and their wives and their families, then you come to an understanding why the thing is for the first place.

Because it's sad as I said to lose a loved one, lying there mouldering under the sea, thinking about them never to be found, never to have a Christian burial. You can't go to their graveside and put flowers round their grave as many people do. But if you were brought up with the idea down through time since childhood, the reason that these people had never been found – they had joined the seal folk and become seal people. And they'll come back again. Because there are many strange stories of people being lost at sea returning five, ten years later. Probably some people say in reality that they hit their head against a stone trying to make their way to the shore after their ship had got into trouble, and by hitting their head against a stone had lost their memory, wandered away and were taken care of by someone. They had a loss of memory and then got their memory back through time; they returned to their homeland and appeared in the village after all these years. But don't tell that to the people, not to the people with the belief! Because they understand, they have been told, 'Someday your loved one will come back.' And they brought all these strange stories of the underworld, stories of the land of the seal people. Some of these are very very strange. So let me tell you a seal story.

It so happened on a little island off the Hebrides many many years ago the love of the people's life was . . . in the springtime of the year they loved to collect eggs, wild birds' eggs, gannets' eggs, the *solan goose* they called them. A Scottish name for it, the old Scotch word, they loved the eggs of the solan goose.

But the little island where the birds found sanctuary was a bird sanctuary, no habitation was on it because it was surrounded by steep, sharp rocks and the weather around it was always bad. But they could only collect eggs at one certain time, in the spring of the year when the birds began to lay. If they overlooked by a week then the eggs would be rotten because the birds would be sitting on them. They had to find a special day, and then they would collect thousands of eggs! But the birds would just lay all over again, they werenae losing anything. Wild goose eggs, divers' eggs, gulls' eggs – all the birds that took sanctuary on the island – their eggs they enjoyed and shared out among the people in the village.

So one day, it was time to go to the island. They thought the weather was going to be calm, a group of them, especially young men from the village, some of the older men too. And this little boat held nine-a-side, rowing. Of course they rowed to the little island, found a place, a kind of sheltery cove where they could beach the boat. And they all spread across the island with their baskets to collect the eggs as many as they could find! There was only one day to do it. If left for the weekend the eggs would be rotten. So they collected eggs all the half-day. And just afore the afternoon would approach and the weather change they made their way to the boat carrying their baskets, packed them all by in the boat thinking about the enjoyment their wives in the village would have when they got their eggs back.

So they rowed back safe and sound. But then, when they shared them out, everybody gathered round to see how many eggs they had collected, they forgot . . . they had left someone on the island – one of the young men of the village. And a storm had arose. They couldn't get back that evening, or the next evening. But on the third day the weather subsided, they managed to get a few men in a boat to row to the island to bring him back.

But when they went there they searched the island over and over and over and over again, but he was gone. They thought he had drowned, was carried away by the tide. He couldn't swim because it was too far, nearly four hours' rowing to get to that little island.

But anyhow, with the sadness in the village there was a sermon held in the church for him and everything else. All the family were upset.

So time passed by and wonst again it was the spring of the year. It would be time, because this was the custom, to gather the eggs as usual. So everybody was warned to see that everyone was aboard the boat before the boat left this time, to leave no one on the island. They took off with their baskets and landed in the same little cove. And to their amazement was a young man standing there, with a long coat coming to his ankles and he had a beard, a blond beard. He was healthy and strong! And they were so excited.

He stood there, he watched them but never lay a hand near an egg. He stood and watched them. And they finally said:

'You've got to come back. Your parents will be overjoyed to see you alive.'

So he said, 'Yes.' And he went with them with his long smooth sealskin coat coming to his ankles.

When he got back they had a gathering in the village, everyone came to welcome him back. And then he told them a strange story. He said he'd met a young woman on the island, a beautiful young woman. And she took care of him for a full year. He stayed with her, he made love to her. And she'd told him before the boat arrived there's a boat coming for him, he was going to be rescued from the island; that's why he was waiting at the little covelet where the boat came in.

But he also told something else that she'd told him: that, at the end of the week at the church there would be a basket appearing in the church from out of nowhere, and he was to tell the local minister – if there were a baby in the basket – the baby should be baptized in the church on the same day it arrived.

So the Sunday came and everyone in the village gathered towards the church waiting to see this miracle happening.

They didn't believe his story, thought he was a little touched in the head after all that year in the island alone. But where did the coat come from?

But as if by magic a basket did appear on the steps of the church covered with a little red shawl, a fishermen's creel basket that carried their hooks and their lines. And she had said to him, if there was a baby in the basket everything was going to be well for him and he was going to have a happy life; but if the basket was empty, then there was trouble in store for him. The minister explained this to the people.

And he walked over, pulled the shawl off the basket and the basket was empty. The young man took one look at the basket and shook his head. He ran and he ran and the people tried to follow him and bring him back but he kept on running. He ran to one part of the village where there was a cliff with a three-hundred-fifty foot drop into the sea, and he threw himself over the cliff into the sea.

So naturally they went round the cliff with a boat to pick up his body, but what they found was the body of a seal. And they brought back the body of the seal. For the body of the man never was found. The coat was gone. It was a seal they found. And the seal was buried in the churchyard with the local people. His name was not put on the stone, but there were some words engraved on the stone. It said SEAL MAN on the stone in the graveyard, and it remains to this very day.

Gull's Eggs

A long time ago in the Western Isles, Jack lived with his mother. She had a little croft well out in the country, far from the nearest village. And there Jack was born and reared up with his mother. He attended a little school in the neighbourhood where he used to walk every morning with a piece of cake or a scone in his pocket for his lunch. And the only thing that Jack really wanted to do was sit and listen, learn as much as he could, and then hurry home. He loved to be home with his mother. There he could help her. She had one single old cow, a few chickens and a couple of goats. And they lived very happy. It was the happiness in Jack's life to escape from school and get home to his mother. He was not interested in education. He only wanted to just read and write.

Because his mother lived about two miles from the little village, she needed to provide for her son while he went to school. The little croft they lived on couldn't produce enough. Jack was too young to work on the croft. There was grass on the place and the little field had been ploughed at one time. But her husband who had died long before when Jack was born had never given much thought to the little place. So there was the old mother and Jack caught in this little croft! Oh, she really tried hard the best she could to bring up her son, send him to school and do all these things for him.

But in his heart and in his head Jack had a burning ambition to know who was his father. Where did his father come from? His mother had never mentioned his father to him. Maybe it was because he was too young she never thought she would bring up the subject of his father. Well, when he came home one evening she said:

'I'm sorry, Jack, I don't have much to give you for supper tonight.'

Jack used to come home and his mother would have oatmeal cakes for him, a bit of cheese and something else, a little homemade meal which the crofting people had in the Western Isles. And the meals were very few and far between, very scarce.

'Well,' she said, 'laddie, to tell you the truth, things are getting awful bad for us.'

He says, 'Why, Mother?'

She said, 'Look, nobody has come and asked me to do any washing for them or do any sewing, any knitting or anything. Jack, things are getting really bad. And look, the cow's going dry. There's no milk for your tea tonight. There's no milk for your porridge in the morning.'

'Ach well, Mother, we can't help that.'

She says, 'Jack, you know you're twelve years old now. You should be able to stand on your own feet and do a wee bit work for me.'

'O Mother, you know I would do anything for you!'

'Look, the morn's Saturday. There's no school. I want you to go to the town the morn, Jack.'

But he says, 'Mother, you say we've no money. We've no money to go to the town with.'

'Well, I'll raik a few coppers up the morn, Jack, and you'll go to the town and get me a wee bit tobacco for my pipe.' She liked to smoke the pipe, the old woman. 'And maybe with the coppers that I have to spare you could maybe buy two-three things, especially oatmeal, to keep us over the weekend.'

So Jack said, 'All right, Mother, the morn's Saturday.'

Now he had to walk across the island about two miles to the local wee store. Because there was only one store. So the next morning after breakfast his mother raiked her purse, and she got a few pennies and a few ha'pennies and farthings. She counted out four shillings. She offered Jack the money and he took it.

'Mother, I don't want to lose it.'

She took out a wee hankie and put it in the handkerchief, tied it in a knot. And she gave him it.

She said, 'Carry this in your hand or put it in your pocket, whatever you want. And remember, Jack, a wee bit tobacco, some oatmeal and some dry tea. I'm no caring what you do with the rest.'

So Jack said goodbye to his mother and walked across the island. But on his travels crossing the main land there was a big rock out from the main land where all the gulls used to lay their eggs. There were many nests out there. Jack had robbed the nests many times for eggs for his and his mother's tea. But when he came up to the wee path that passed it this day Jack was lucky – the tide was out. So he walked along the path. But who was sitting there but an old man with a long beard down to his chin!

This old man had a piece of cardboard or cloth. He was painting. He was an artist or something. And he was drawing all this, painting the island, you see!

But when he came up to the old man Jack said, 'Hello!'

The old man looked up, 'Hello, young man.' He never paid much attention.

But Jack stood and watched for a wee while. When Jack

looked, what was the old man doing? He had about four or five gull's eggs with their tops broken off. And Jack had never seen anything like this before in his life, these gulls' eggs broken off. And the old man had poured off the white of each egg, and he had the yolk mixed up inside the shell. He was painting all these beautiful pictures, dooking a wee brush into the gull's eggs. Jack had never seen anyone do this before because he'd never met an artist. So he stood and watched the old man making circles over the sea and the wee island, and all the things that he was making.

The old man said, 'Are you interested, son, in what I'm doing?'

Jack said, 'What are you doing?'

He said, 'I'm a painter.'

'Oh, I see you're a painter,' Jack says. 'But what are you doing making paints with the gull's eggs? I dinnae ken much about paint, mister, but is it no a sin that you should make a painting with the wee gull's eggs? You stole the wee gull's eggs from the nests to make paint.'

'Och, it's only gull's eggs,' he said.

But Jack said to him, 'Do you no think that these wee gulls had an awful problem laying these eggs? And that's their babies. You're destroying their wee eggs making a painting from their eggs! And I don't think that's very nice. Can you no get some paint, some colouring?'

'No, my son,' he says, 'go away! Go away, leave me in peace. Go on, go on!'

'Well,' Jack said, 'I'm going on. But I'm no very happy about what you're doing.'

'Be on with you, be on! Leave me at peace!'

But Jack walked on. He left the old man, thinking about these gulls' eggs. And on he goes to the shop, to the wee village. He goes into the shop, and there's an old woman behind the store with a sheet apron on her, you see, and a mutch on her head, a wee bonnet.

Now this old woman was never married in her life. And because she owned the local store she knew all the gossip in the village. In fact, she knew everyone. She knew every date of birth of every child who was born. She knew the post man. She knew everyone! There was nothing that old Maggie didn't know. Nothing old Maggie doesn't know! So Jack put his hankie on the top of the table.

'Well, Jack!' she says. She kent him well. 'How's your mother?'

'No bad, Maggie,' he says. 'She's keeping fine.'

He called her Maggie; he was allowed to call her by her first name because she was a very good friend. He came and visited often.

And she says, 'What can I do for you?'

He says, 'My mother wants tea, tobacco and oatmeal.'

And he put the coppers on the table. She selected what she needed.

She says, 'Jack, you look awfae solemn.'

'Aye, well, Maggie, to tell you the truth, when I was coming down this morning from my mother's croft I came across the path by the island, the rock. The tide was out.'

'Aye,' she says, 'laddie.'

'And, there was an old man sitting there. He was painting and making impressions.'

'Aye, Jack, he's been here in the village. He's an Englishman.'

'Well, I thought he was by his accent. I couldn't understand him very well.' Because Jack was used to Gaelic and Scots. 'But, Maggie,' he said, 'do you no think it's a sin . . . look, he's painting with the wee gulls' eggs from the island!'

She said, 'Jack, you've collected eggs many's a time yourself.

'Aye, Maggie, I've collected eggs many's a time myself. I never collected eggs for to put them on paper and make a fool of them and break them up, mix up wee yokes! Me and my mother like a wee gull's egg to eat or a dooker's egg or a scarf's or another wild bird's egg. But I only take *one* from the nest. And he's sitting painting there!'

She says, 'Jack, are you upset about this?'

'Aye, Maggie!'

Now, old Maggie had never any weans of her own. None of her own. And to her Jack was her favourite. Of all the weans in the village Jack was her favourite. Jack was always kind and nice and treated her with respect. Sometimes he called her auntie, sometimes old Maggie.

She says, 'Jack, what would you like to do about it?'

'Well,' he says, 'I'm no very happy about it, Auntie Maggie, I'm no very happy. That man can come from all that distance and sit anywhere in the country, take all the wee gulls' eggs from the island, break them up and mix their wee yolks and paint pictures from them!'

'Oh well, Jack, you're upset are you?'

'Aye, I'm really upset. I wouldn't mind if somebody would come and take the gull's eggs like ourselves.'

'Aye,' she said, 'you ay bring me two or three for my tea. And I like them!'

But he says, 'No that, Maggie. I always bring *one* from the nest, never three. I don't clean the nest out. I only bring one and leave the rest to grow up.'

She said, 'Aye, Jack, you're a good laddie! Well, maybe I could help you.'

'Well, Aunt Maggie, I'm no very happy about it. I wish you would help me.'

'Well, I'll tell you what I'll do,' she said. 'You pack up your mother's wee bit messages. And it's a long time since I've seen your mother. It'll soon be closing time. I'll be closing the shop about three o'clock. And I want to see your mother anyway because I've never seen her for years. She's a good chum o' mine. And I'll walk back with you.'

'O Aunt Maggie, that would be nice! It would be good if you would come and see her.' So Jack packed up his mother's wee bits o' messages in a wee paper bag.

And she says, 'Come on then, I'll close the shop! There's nobody else about.'

She went and locked the back door. She got her coat, and with the mutch on her head she locked the front door:

'Come on, laddie, we'll go.'

But the sun was still high in the sky. They walked back the path. Jack with the wee brown poke below his oxter with his mother's tea and meal and bit tobacco and the old woman with the mutch, they walked on.

She said, 'Dinnae travel too fast, I cannae keep up with you!' Because Jack was only twelve years old and she was maybe in her sixties.

When they came along, sure enough there was the old man with the beard on him sitting by the rock. And he had his painting set before him. He had another four gull's eggs. When they came up they stopped.

And after he painted he waited for a few moments. Then he stopped and looked up.

He said, 'Well, what can I do for youse? What do youse want?'

Jack said, 'This is my auntie and she runs the store.' Well, it wasn't his auntie but he called her this. 'She runs the store and she wants to see what you're doing, the thing you're making with the gull's eggs.'

He said, 'She's welcome to look if she wants to.'

And the old woman looked round about. She saw the picture, the painting. It was the island and all the gulls flying over the top of the island. It was half finished. The old woman came round and she looked. Old Maggie looked at the gull's eggs a long, long time. Then she looked again at the painting. She said to the man who was painting the picture:

'Dae ye see that picture you're makkin? It's no richt.'

And he said, 'What do you know about painting, old woman?'

'Oh,' she said, 'that gull is not fleein right. That gull up in that corner is not fleein right.'

He said, 'Do you think you could do better?'

'Aye,' she said, 'I could.'

And she crossed her two hands *like that*. She rubbed her hands together. And the picture took off from the easel. Off it went and on and on – off it went and vanished, dropped into the sea!

The old man stood in amazement. He said, 'Woman, what have you done to me? Why did you destroy my picture?'

She says, 'I have not destroyed your picture. *You have destroyed all the gulls on the island!*'

And she says, 'Come on, Jack, we'll go and see your mother.' As she was walking away she picked up two gull's eggs that weren't broken, and she said, 'We'll take these, Jack, to your mother's tonight. And we'll bring them back, put them back in the nest in the morning.'

God rest Uncle Duncan told me that story. Uncle Duncan was Granny's favourite. He was born and reared up with her. And when he married he still stayed with her, kept her along with him.

So Uncle Duncan would say, 'I'll tell you a story, weans!'

Old Granny would interfere and say, 'That's no the way it goes.'

Now he said it was his story. But she told it to him first, and he told it from her telling.

A Silkieman

Living on an island you had only one option and that's to make a living by the sea. And there are so many strange tales, many tragedies where people live on islands, not only in Scotland or England or Ireland, but all over the world; strange stories about things happening at sea. Even in Japan there are sea spirits and evil spirits. But especially in the West Coast among the Gaelic speaking people of Scotland there are great legends of things that they believe in . . . when someone *believes* in something deep in their soul, they believe in reality.

This story begins with a fisherman and his son who lived on a little island in the Hebrides. Fishermen, not with big trawlers or motor boats but inshore fishermen, they fished with lines from their boats and depended on their lines for to catch as much food as they could. What they could not keep for theirself they sold. And at night-time, when he was a little, small boy his father, when his wife was busy, would tell his son many strange stories about tales of the sea people, the silkies, and tragedies just for the sake of passing away the evening like my father used to tell us when I was small. And one strange story he told his son exists with us today.

He said, 'You know, boy, I'm going to tell you a true story.'

'Daddy,' he said, 'your stories are not true. They're just made up.'

'No, my son, they're not made up. They're passed down from tradition and I'm going to tell you a story that happened to me. Just like you, my boy, my father used to tell me strange stories when I was a little boy too; but I didn't believe him either, the way you don't believe me. But this happened to me! I'm no asking you to believe me but you know I wouldn't lie to you, my little son.'

'Tell me the story, father!' And the little boy seemed to get excited because he loved his father telling a story, like I used to tell Thomas when he was a little boy.

'You see, well, it happened, my boy, some years ago, long before you were born. We used to go out fishing with our boats every day, but we had a tradition that we never took wir boats on the beach. We always tied wir boats up and left them floating. There was a little rope, you could pull them in in the afternoon, pull them in at night when we felt like it. No one beached their boat. But one day I was out fishing with my drag lines over the boat . . .' which is hand lines; you just rowed out to a deep part of the sea and then threw all your lines over the side. You waited, and you pulled them up, maybe ten lines over each side of the boat.

And he said, 'I threw my lines out and I'm sitting waiting. You always give the fish an hour anyway to come along and take your bait. When lo and behold the next thing I saw was the water breaking and up beside the boat, boy, comes a head, not a head of a seal but the strangest head I've ever seen in my life. With its big brown eyes it looks up to me and I was mesmerized, I didn't know what to do.'

The wee boy's sitting watching his daddy.

The father said, 'Boy, it was a *seal man*!'

'A seal man, Daddy?'

'It was a seal man, boy! It was half seal and half human. And putting its hand across its chest it said, "I'm cold, I'm cold, my hands are cold, my hands are cold, help me!" Hoo could I help? I didn't know what to do. The only thing I had', he said, 'were these big leather gloves. And all I could do was take my gloves off and just throw them to him. I threw my gloves and they landed in the water, and he picked one up and he picked the other one up. And he disappeared! Now, boy, this is true, I'm telling you the truth. The bubbles came up and he was gone. And I waited and I waited for a whole day. My hands were cold, but his hands were a lot colder than mine. And he was gone!

'But I had a nice afternoon's fishing, my boy, really a good night. I caught many fishes that day and I took them home. What your mother couldn't use I took to the village and sold. And the rest of the fishermen returned, they didn't have as good a day as I had. We all tied up wir boats naturally as we always done. And of course we went to wir bed.

'But during the night something wakened me, something disturbed my sleep, and I heard something calling through the window, "The night is dark, the night is cold, the wind's going to blow tonight, and no ship shall be safe in the water tonight!" On and on it went, "The night is dark, the night is cold and no ship shall be safe in the water tonight."

'Boy,' he said, 'I knew that voice, I knew that was no human telling me my boat was in danger. So I dressed myself and I hurried down to the beach and I pulled in my little boat high and dry, safe from the tide. And you know, boy, there on the back seat were my gloves! I still have them to this day. And that night there came the worst storm that ever raged across the island, and the boats that were in the water that night were smashed to pieces. But my boat was safe all because I befriended *a silkieman.'*

The Genie and the Fisherman

I heard this story from an old traveller when I was about fourteen, when we used to gather together and tell old stories. The travellers in those days had hundreds and hundreds and hundreds of stories – and this very old tale is supposed to have been true.

There was once an old fisherman and his wife and they lived by the side of the shore. He was very poor and used to go out every morning – it was a hand net he used for casting from the shore. In those old-fashioned days the fishermen threw nets out into the sea to try and catch some fish. But things began to get very hard for them and the more he fished the less he got. Every time he came back his wife would shout and argue with him:

'You are a poor fisherman, ye cannae catch nothing! What are we going to live on, how are we going to survive? You must try yer best, rise up early in the morning and go out and catch some decent fish! So we can sell some and have some to ourselves.'

And the poor old man did his level best. Every day he rose at day-break and fished till dark. Some days he got nothing. And whenever he came home without any fish his wife would shout and argue and scold at him, tell him how useless as a fisherman he was, how they were going to survive she didn't know. She told him he would just have to keep on trying.

So one morning he swore to himself, 'I am going down to fish this morning and I am not going to come back until I make it worthwhile!'

He cast his net in the sea and he fished, and he fished all day and still got nothing. He was just getting fed up when he thought, 'I will have one more go. I'll go along the beach a bit where I have never fished before and try.'

And he cast his net once again, waited till it sank into the water. He pulled his net in . . . but nothing, not one single fish in the net.

But right in the corner of the net was an old-fashioned bottle, the oldest-fashioned clay bottle he had ever seen in his life. It was covered in seaweed it was so old! And the old man pulled his net, pulled it up on the beach and lifted out the bottle.

He looked round the bottle, and round the bottle, and said to himself, 'I've never seen a bottle like this before in my life . . . it must be very old . . . I wonder if there is anything in it?'

He never knew what it was meant for – there was an old glass, a kind of stone cork in it. And he took his old knife out of his pocket, picked the cork off. He put his nose to smell it to see what kind of stuff was in it, when out of the bottle came the smoke – dark, dark smoke! And the old man was afraid.

The smoke got bigger and bigger and rose in a cloud above his head. It began to take form . . . it turned into a genie, a real genie. And the old man was awful feart, oh, he was terrified. The genie spoke to him in a stern voice:

'Old man, do you know what you have done?'

'No, no,' the old man said, 'no, I don't know what I have

done – I never did any harm! I just caught this bottle in my net and I pulled it in, I wanted to see what was inside the bottle. I took off the cork and now you have come out of it! What are ye?'

And the genie said, 'I am a genie! I am the Genie of This Bottle, and for seven hundred years I have been a prisoner in here! I was put in this bottle by my master, who was jealous of me hundreds of years before, and cast out into the sea. There I lay until you picked me up in yer net.

'For the first three hundred years I promised that the person who would take the bottle and let me out, I would make him the richest man in the world, I would give him gold and diamonds and silver for evermore. And still no one took me out. For the second three hundred years I promised that I would make the man the king upon this land, I would give him everything that his heart desired if he would only rescue me from the sea. But still no one picked me out of the sea. Then the last hundred years I swore that whoever took me out of the sea, I would kill him and make him so small – I would put *him* back in the bottle and throw *him* in the sea to suffer what I suffered. *So you are the one!* You are the one to set me free. So I am sorry, old man, but I have to kill you and put yer remains back in the bottle.'

'Well,' the old man said, 'I suppose if you are going to kill me and put me back in the bottle, there is not much I can do about it – seeing you are a big powerful genie, more powerful than me. But before ye do that to me, will ye do one thing for me?'

'Yes,' said the genie, 'I'll do anything for ye. But don't ask me to go back in the bottle!'

'No,' the old man said, 'I'm not asking ye to go back in the bottle, I'm only wondering . . .'

'And what are ye wondering?' said the genie.

'That a person as big as you could come out of that small bottle . . . I can't believe it no way, that a person as large as you could come out of that bottle so small. So just to see that ye are telling me the truth, would ye do me one favour before ye kill me?'

'Well,' said the genie, 'I will grant ye that.'

'Would ye just show me how ye managed to get in that bottle?'

And the genie said, 'Well, just to ease yer mind – before I put ye in the bottle and put ye back in the sea for the rest of the days of yer life – I'll show ye . . .'

And the genie went into a long strip of smoke, he went back into the bottle slowly, slowly, slowly, till every part of him disappeared in the bottle.

Then the old man ran and he put the cork back into the bottle, screwed it tight with his knife. He catcht it and threw it as far as he could out into the sea! And there the bottle lies for the rest of time.

But if ye are walking by the shore and ye see a bottle lying, just be very careful when ye lift it. Because ye never know – it might be the genie in that bottle!

So, not to be beaten, the old man said, 'Well, that was bad luck for me, but I'll have another shot again,' and he cast his net once more.

Lo and behold, he could hardly pull it in it was so loaded with fish! He counted the fish – there were twenty-one fish in his net.

And he carried them all back to his wife. His wife was so happy that she cooked some for him and some for herself and made the old man go to the village, sell the rest of them next morning for some money.

And the funny thing was – from that day on the old man and his wife never had another bad day. Every day the old man went to fish and cast his net off the shore, sure enough there never was a day he threw his net in the sea that he never caught some fish! And he said to himself:

'Maybe,' he said, 'the genie did bring me luck!'

And what do you think then, did the genie bring him good luck or did the genie bring him bad luck? Because I think the genie brought him good luck!

And that's the last of my wee story.

Return of the Silkie

This story took place in one of the islands off the Hebrides . . . but now the thing about the silkie stories when you hear them told the teller never gives the name of the island because it's too close to the people; in case they say you might be telling a lie, this never happened in our island. So they always say in a little island in the Hebrides, and this began a long time ago.

There was a fisherman by the name of Iain Cameron, and Iain Cameron was married to a little woman called Mary. He had a little cottage by the sea. His father had been lost at sea when he was a little boy. But Iain was a terrible man. Mary worked in the local bakery and she was a good cook and a good baker, but her life was a misery because Iain her husband was a terrible man to live with. When he went to the village at the weekends he wouldnae take her with him. He would go to the local hotel and call the old men 'crows' and the old women 'hags'. Nobody liked him in the village. He was hated, they couldnae stand him in any way! And poor Mary's life was a torture; because it didna matter if she was good to him – she loved him. He was a good looking man. And he was a good fisherman, always took back plenty fish when he went out. But the people of the village hated him. Mary was threatening many times in her own mind to run away and leave him, but she always stuck her ground. Then one time there was an awful tragedy. One night he never came back.

And she was so alarmed she went to the village and reported he was missing. The local people took out their boats to search for him, but all they found was his upturned little inland boat. Iain Cameron was never found. He was gone.

So she lived alone in her little cottage by herself for one year, still working away in the little local bakery shop. And then one night out of the blue, as if out of nowhere, the door opened and in walked her husband with a long coat coming to his ankles.

She was startled, she says, 'Iain, it's not you is it?'

'Yes,' he said, 'Mary, it's me.' And he smiled at her.

She says, 'Sit you down.'

'Yes,' he said, 'I thank you.' And she brought him a cup of tea.

She says, 'Iain, where have you been?'

He says, 'I haven't been anywhere.'

She says, 'You know it's a year since you've been gone. What happened to you?'

He says, 'Nothing.'

He wouldnae talk to her, he wouldnae explain about it. But he was so gentle and so kind. And now he would take her with him to the village, he would buy her presents; but he always seemed to have plenty money. And it was a new Iain! He was quiet, he was gentle, he was kind, he always smiled. They didnae have any family.

And now she was more disturbed than she was when he was wicked. And he had this coat, this long sealskin coat. And she asked him where he got it.

He said, 'I just got it around.'

But everywhere he went he would put that coat on. When he went to the village, he would step aside and let the old men past. He would buy them a drink, put a handful of gold coins on the bar and a drink for everybody. He would help the old ladies across the street. And this disturbed her so much, the change in her husband.

But she had an old friend whom she used to visit and take cakes and biscuits to, an old woman. And people thought this old woman was kind of strange, a kind of a witch. She was an old herbalist. So one day while Iain was off in the village helping someone to do something she went to visit her old friend. And she told her.

'I've heard about the return of your husband,' said the old woman. 'The news has spread fast and wide.'

So Mary explained to her, 'He's been gone for a year, lost at sea.'

And the old woman hummed and hawed for a little minute, she says, 'How did he come back? How does he look?'

She said, 'He's kind, he's gentle – not the same man he was when he left a year ago – he just treats me like a lady! And he's always got plenty money.'

And the old woman said, 'How did he come back? What was he wearing?'

She said, 'A long fur coat.'

'What did you say?' says the old woman.

She said, 'A long fur coat.'

'Oh I see,' said the old woman. 'Well, if you want to keep your husband, what you'll have to do,' she said, 'is take that coat sometime when he leaves it behind, and burn it!'

She said, 'I can't burn my husband's coat; he loves it, he loves that coat! What would he do to me if he found I burned it?'

She said, 'He'll do nothing. He'll not harm you in any way.'

So for the sake of this she hummed and hawed and thought about it. And then one day he went off to the village and left the coat. Mary took the scissors and she clipped the coat up, burned it in the fire till it was nothing but cinders left of the sealskin coat.

Anyway, he came home and looked behind the door – his coat was gone. He never said one single word, never even asked her if she'd seen it! The funny thing was, he never mentioned the coat anymore.

So she visited her old friend wonst again when he was off and she told her she'd burned the coat.

She said, 'How did he react?'

'He reacted more gentle than he ever did before, he never even asked me about it!'

She says, 'I thought that would happen.'

'Tell me, old woman, tell me, what's wrong, what's wrong with my husband? Why has he changed so much? Who is he? He's not the man I used to know.'

She said, 'Your husband is a *silkie*, a seal man.'

'My husband can't be a seal man!'

'Your husband is a seal man,' she said.

And Mary lived with Iain for many years, and he never as much as called her a liar. They bought another house in the village and moved up there. They never had any family. And Iain became well loved and well respected in the village, helped everybody. But he never mentioned the coat again.

When they were an old couple Mary took sick, and after a short illness she died. He buried her in the local village beside many of their old friends. And one day he closed the house, walked away to the sea. There was only one thought in his mind, he was going back to his people. Mary had no more need for him. She was gone to another place.

But he had to return; because now he was an old man he had to become a seal wonst again. And he had to give his skin before he died to be made into a coat, so it would bring happiness to somebody else in the future.

And that's a true story. Before seals die they give their skins to be made into coats. Seals of the underworld donate their skins, it's an old tradition. That's why they have the power, why the silkies wear these long coats made from the skins of their forefathers. When an old seal gets ready to die they give their skin to be made into coats that they can give to the young. And once you wear a sealskin coat you'll never be the same person again. Iain knew he had to become a seal, go back to the underworld of the seal people and give up his skin to be made into a coat, so that it could be used to give happiness to someone else in the future. And that's the story.

It was told to me by the old man in Clachan, an old farmer MacDougall of Dunscaig, the old man who told me the Silkie Painter – that was his story, came from the same person.

Shell House

John MacDougall in Dunscaig Farm beside Clachan lived with his wife and his maid, and he had a couple of sisters who lived in the village. I got a couple of weeks' employment with him when I'd left home at the age of thirteen and travelled down the west coast of Kintyre. I was staying in the barn, and I worked with John. I respected the old man very much. He's long gone, dead now. Maybe some of his relations are still around. And one evening I was sitting in an old corn kist. I had a little bed in the barn where I stayed. John came in and we sat there and talked for a while. I was telling him about my search for stories:

'Well,' he said, 'there's some stories I've heard myself.'

I said, 'John, if I were to tell you a story, would you tell me a story?'

'Well,' he said, 'I've never told any stories, Duncan, but this is one that my grandmother used to tell a long time ago. When me and my little sisters were very small we used to listen to our grandmother telling a story.'

And this is the story he told me.

In a little village a long time ago on the West Coast there once lived a young woman called Margaret MacKay. Margaret MacKay's father was the local grave-digger. In his spare time he was a beadle of the church, pulling the bell and taking care of the church. And Margaret's mother had died when she was very small. She attended the local village school. And of course Margaret spent most of her time – because the cottage that they lived in was beside the sea – her love was collecting all those beautiful shells. Shells of all descriptions, of all the little creatures she could find. And of course she placed them around her house. It was known to the local villagers as Shell House.

The people knew Margaret's obsession for shells. When they came for a visit, they had to walk down an old rough road leading from the local village to the house by the seaside where Margaret lived with her father. And Margaret would spend many evenings along the beach that stretched for miles. There were many beautiful coves in the bay where she would wander while her daddy was taking care of the graveyard and looking after the church. Margaret was very happy. But the happiness in her life was taking care of her shells.

Even though her father was a gravedigger they kept a large amount of ducks and hens. That was all the animals they had and Margaret took care of them. But then, when she was in her twenties her father died and left her all alone. Of course Margaret continued to carry on with her life as usual. She lived all alone, but would bring her eggs to the village. She would take them to the local store.

Now in the local store was a man named Angus MacDonald. Angus had been in school with Margaret. And his father had died when Angus was very small. But Angus's mother was still alive. And Angus's mother had a great love for Margaret. She was always telling Angus:

'Such a wonderful young woman, Angus! How could you not marry her?'

And he would say, 'Mother, of course, why should I marry the young woman? We were in school together and she has no affection, no love for me. We are just good friends.'

Now the thing about Angus, he lived with his mother in this small village, he ran the local post office in the local store where the people came for their little groceries. But Angus was kind of mean. He loved money, was very fond of it. He went out of his way to make a penny, or make a shilling. And each day after he closed the store – he had a little house attached to the post office – he would make his mother a cup of tea. She was a very old woman was Angus' mother. And everything she brought up in the conversation was about Margaret, Margaret MacKay.

'Angus, she's such a beautiful woman. Why don't you and her get closer?'

'Mother,' she's just a good friend of mine. And of course you can't just go and ask a young lady to marry you or something!'

Now the village was not very large. The local villagers knew all about Angus's mother's obsession for Margaret. But not so with Angus MacDonald; as far as he was concerned Margaret was only his school mate.

But anyhow, not far from the village was a large house where a laird lived who owned most of the village and the land all around. And Angus would always take eggs to the big house. But it happened Angus would try his best to skin a fly for a penny, as we call it on the West Coast. Because Angus was greedy. He never helped anyone in the village in any way. I mean, the old folk were poor. He would just try and cheat them as much as he could. But his mother was an old darling lady. And of course everyone knew her. But she didn't come out very much. Here my story begins.

Two days, three days passed and Margaret never turned up at the store. And Angus was completely out of eggs when he got a message from the big house, the laird's house on the hill. They were having some kind of party, a birthday meeting together and they needed some eggs. Now it was late in the evening when word arrived. And the eggs were badly needed at the big house. So Angus said:

'Mother, I've had a message from the big house. I'll have to walk down to Margaret's tonight to see if she has any eggs. I can walk down myself.' Now it was about a mile down the old rough track leading to the beach and Margaret's cottage, surrounded by shells.

'Well,' she said, 'it's a very cold night. Take your coat with you.'

'Och no, Mother,' he said, 'I'll not need a coat. I'll just take my scarf.'

He wrapped the scarf round his neck. And he walked down. The road was not very good and not used for anything. Vehicles could never go down the road that led to Margaret's house.

And as he came down – he had not come to Margaret's house very often, but he'd been there once or twice – he saw that every single window of the house was lighted. Angus thought this was very strange. Because Margaret had only kept one little room lit, one light on in the kitchen when he'd visited her previously. But tonight the house was in a lunary of lights. It was paraffin lamps. And Angus came up.

Now there was a large bay window that faced the shore. This was the kitchen area. And when Angus came along he looked in through the window. The curtains were parted. And there to his amazement he could see a large number of people sitting with Margaret. Margaret was in the middle and she was busy talking away.

Angus stood for a few minutes. And he thought to himself, 'Who could this be? Where did these people come from?' And then he remembered . . . 'Maybe it's tinkers,' he said.

Margaret always catered for the local tinkers when they came through the village. She always gave them eggs and was very good to them.

But Angus said, 'I've never seen any tinkers in the village for a while. It can't be tinkers.'

So he went up to the door and he knocked. And he waited. Then Margaret came to the door:

'Hello, Angus, what is it?'

'Margaret, excuse me for bothering you. But I've just got word from the big house – I'm needing some eggs.'

'Oh,' she said, 'I see. But I was so busy that I couldn't get up with the eggs. I've got plenty.'

'Well, I'm needing about three dozen for the big house. Margaret, who's all the people?'

'Och, Angus, it's some friends of mine.'

'Friends, Margaret?' he said. 'What . . . are they local tinkers or something?'

'No, no, Angus, it's no tinkers at all. It's some friends.'

'But Margaret, where did . . . are they from the village?'

'No, no, Angus,' she says, 'they're not from the village. They're just some friends of mine.'

And because the wind was blowing it was very cold and she couldn't have him standing at the door, she said, 'Angus, you'd better come in!'

She brought him into the little kitchen in the house. And sitting around were about fifteen people. Angus looked all around.

But Margaret had gone in before him, and as he closed the door behind he felt something soft hanging on the back of the door. A coat, a beautiful coat, it felt so soft. Angus closed the door without using the handle. He just pushed it. And there was the long, soft coat hanging behind the door. Angus's hand sank into the coat.

When he walked into the room Margaret said: 'Excuse me, friends, but we have a visitor.'

And all these people looked up. Angus looked. He saw the strangest set of people he ever saw in his life. Because everyone looked identical. They were all round-faced . . . wonderful looking people! And they all had these beautiful brown eyes.

And Margaret was saying, 'Excuse me, friends, but my visitor has come to call. I'm sorry.'

'Oh,' one of the men sitting in the corner says, 'you've no need to be sorry, Margaret. Any friend of yours is a friend of ours.'

And he stood up and Angus could see that everyone was dressed in a long coat, the same identical coat. Everyone was dressed the same way.

And the one who stood, the largest one said, 'Welcome, friend!'

And Angus shook hands with him: 'I'm Angus MacDonald from the village and I've come for some eggs.'

'Oh,' he said, 'don't let us interfere with you.'

'Oh, it's no problem.'

He says, 'You'd better sit down then and rest yourself.'

Margaret said, 'I'll go and get you your eggs, Angus,' and she filled a basket.

Angus looked around. There were young people, there were old people. There were people middle-aged. About fifteen of them.

Then Margaret came forward and she said: 'Angus, I'm sorry. But you could stay!'

'Oh no, I can't stay, Margaret. I'm really sorry. I've got to hurry back because the laird in the big house needs his eggs.' He said, 'I'm sorry, people, but I have to go!'

Not one spoke except this particular man. He stood up and said:

'Angus, you're walking home to the village tonight. It's kind of cold. *Take my coat.*'

'Oh,' Angus said, 'I could not take your coat.'

'Yes, Angus, please take my coat. You're a friend of Margaret's, you're a friend of mine!' And he took off his coat. He held it open: 'Now it's a long, cold way home. Put this on you!'

And Angus said, 'Well, I thank you very much. In a little while I'll return it.'

'Oh no,' he says, 'don't return it to me. You keep it! I have another.'

Angus slipped into this coat. It was warm and comfortable and went down to his heels. It felt like fur but it was not fur. It was the strangest coat. But when Angus put it on he felt very strange . . . he felt his heart light. His heart became light. He wanted to stay with these people:

'Who were these people?' thought Angus.

And then Margaret came in with the basket of eggs and she said, 'Here you are, Angus! Will I see you again?'

'Well,' he says, 'I'll see you tomorrow maybe, Margaret. Good night, Margaret. I'm sorry for interrupting your friends.'

'O Angus, don't you worry.'

But he says, 'Margaret, will you tell me, are they tinkers?'

'No, no no, Angus, they're not tinkers. They're my friends.'

But he says, 'Where have they come from?'

'Angus, I have to tell you. But will you promise me faithfully?'

'Margaret,' he said, 'you know you and I have been in school with each other together. I promise you anything within reason!'

'Angus, will you promise you will never tell a soul as long as you live? Have I got your promise?'

'Margaret, you and I've been friends since our childhood. I promise you anything!'

She says, 'Angus, they're *seal people*.'

'Ach, Margaret, there's no such a thing as seal people!'

'Yes, Angus,' she says, 'there are seal people. They're my friends, and they've come for a visit.'

'But Margaret, they all look alike.'

'Yes, they all look alike. And they're my friends. But anyhow, Angus, I'll maybe see you tomorrow if I have time.'

'But, Margaret,' he said, 'there's no such a thing as seal people!'

'Angus, now listen to me carefully: one of them has given you his coat. You take care of that coat! Look after it and you will feel better with it.'

Angus walked away with his basket of eggs. Angus walked home with the basket in his hand. And he was whistling to himself. He felt comfortable. He felt strange. He felt happy. Some kind of lightness had gone to his heart. And he was thinking mostly of Margaret:

'Such a wonderful woman. My mother is right. She is a beautiful lady.'

And when he walked home to the little store where he lived with his mother he went in and put the eggs on the table. His mother was sitting knitting by the fireside on her old rocking chair. And she looked up.

She said, 'Angus, you're back.'

'Yes, Mother, I'm back.'

'Did you get the eggs from Margaret? How was she?'

'Oh,' he says, 'Margaret . . . Mother, she's fine.'

And then she said, 'Angus, where did you get the coat?'

'Mother, I borrowed it from' . . . now he didn't want to tell. 'I borrowed it from Margaret. It must have been her father's.'

'No, Angus, that's not her father's coat. You're taller than her father. I knew old John well. But he never had a coat like that in all his time. That's a . . . come over closer to me till I feel it.'

And he walked over, and the old woman reached over. She groped it with her hand.

She said, 'Angus, that's the most beautiful thing I've ever seen! Where did you get it?'

He said, 'I borrowed it from Margaret. Because it was kind of cold when I left the house.'

'And how is the dear girl?'

'Oh, she's fine!'

'Angus, wouldn't she make a wonderful wife?'

'Och, Mother, of course she'd make a wonderful wife. But she doesn't want anything to do with me!'

'Angus, it's the only thing that would make me happy – if you and Margaret were to get together. Because I'll not be with you for very long, you know, I'm getting old and my time is nearly come.'

'Ach, Mother, behave yourself!' But he started to sing in the house!

And his old mother's looking, and she said: 'Angus, what's come over you?'

'Och, Mother, I feel fine tonight.'

She says, 'Angus, I think I know what's happened to you. You're in love!'

'Well, Mother, maybe I am!' he said.

So he took his coat off and he hung it behind the door. But from that moment on Angus became a changed man.

Margaret visited the old woman because she visited Angus's mother at least once a week. She would sit and have a cup of tea with her.

But Angus' mother's only thing was . . . 'And what do you think of Angus now then? Isn't he a handsome . . .'

'Ach,' she said, 'Angus is fine. He's a good friend of mine.'

But Angus became a changed man. And because Angus changed, within a few days Margaret began to see this in him. He was happy! He was whistling, he was singing. He was serving the store. And then Margaret began to hear after she returned to her cottage what wonderful work Angus was doing for the old people in the village. He was helping everyone. He was good to everyone.

And one day Angus put on his coat and he walked down to Margaret's house. When he came there Margaret was busy washing eggs. You know eggs get dirty sometimes! And he had his coat on. He was smiling, whistling to himself.

He says, 'Margaret, I've come to ask you a question.'

'Yes, Angus?'

'Would you care to walk with me?' And he had his long coat on.

'Where would you like to walk, Angus?'

He said, 'I would like to walk along the beach.'

'Well, wait and I'll get my coat.'

And Margaret went behind the door and she took down the coat. The very coat that he'd put his hand against when he'd felt it – identical to the one that he owned, that was given to him.

She says, 'Angus, do you like your coat?'

'O Margaret, I love my coat! But I love something more than my coat. I love you, Margaret! Margaret,' he said, 'would you marry me?'

'Well, Angus, I've been waiting for that for a long, long
time.'

'Have you?'

'Of course, Angus,' she said. 'You're not the same person.'

'No, Margaret, I'm not the same person I was a long time
ago. I think I'm in love.' [And I swear over my mother's
grave as he sat there back in 1941, I can see him smiling –
old John MacDougall's face as he sat there. He was probably
thinking of his own love in years.] And as they walked along
the beach he asked her again, would she marry him?

She says, 'Yes, I've been waiting for that for a long time.'

But anyhow, they came home and sat and talked. Margaret
had promised she would marry Angus MacDonald.

So, to make a long story short there was a small wedding
in the village. Everyone in the village was interested and
excited. Angus MacDonald was marrying Margaret MacKay
in the village church. Of course, the local minister was there.
And everybody wanted to see the beautiful bride dressed
for the occasion. Everyone turned up at the church who was
invited.

But to the amazement of everyone, Angus and Margaret
appeared in two long coats at the church! Two long, black
coats down to their feet. And everyone gazed and stared.
Where were the beautifully dressed bride and groom?
But they could see the faces of Angus and Margaret were
blossoming in happiness just dressed as they were. There
was a small, quiet wedding and Angus and Margaret were
married. A small reception in the village, and everyone
turned up. But to the amazement of everyone – Angus and
Margaret wouldn't take off their coats – for no one breathing!

So, a few days later Angus got a young man to run the
store for him. And he went to live with Margaret in her little
cottage by the seaside. And of course his old mother, she

was just over the moon, over the moon! This is what she wanted all her life. Now she could die in peace.

So everyone was wondering, even the local minister, why Margaret and Angus were so happy? Why hadn't they dressed for a great wedding in the church?

But anyhow, within a few weeks Angus's mother died. There was a great sermon. And to the amazement of everyone, Angus and Margaret turned up to the sermon dressed in their long coats as usual. And this of course made the local villagers think again about the change that had come over Angus MacDonald. For Angus was happy – he was the happiest man of all. And three weeks after his mother had died he sold the store to the local man who had run it for him. And he and Margaret lived happily in their little cottage by the shore.

But sometimes Margaret would hire a young man to take care of her hens and her ducks for her. Because they would go off on a journey to visit friends. They were gone for many weeks. And people often wondered where Margaret and Angus had gone. Because no one knew exactly who their friends were. And they would say:

'I wonder when Angus and Margaret will be coming back again.'

Whenever they appeared in the village they always appeared in their long coats. Whenever they walked along the beach they always appeared in long coats. And Angus and Margaret didn't have any children. They lived very happily in the little Shell House till their old age.

In her late seventies Margaret died. The local minister was a dear friend of theirs. When Angus came to him he said:

'Minister, when I die bury me beside Margaret. And there's Margaret's coat; and you'll get mine when I die.'

So after a few years Angus finally died. And of course the minister kept his promise; he would bury Angus's coat with him as he had done with Margaret's.

But then for some strange reason, before the funeral service for Angus he took down the coat from a peg where it hung. And he put his hand in the pocket. He brought out a little red book. And he sat down, he looked at it.

He said, 'This is very strange. This is a strange, strange story.'

The minister read the story from the little red book that was found in Angus' pocket. And Angus was buried beside his wife with his coat. And the minister kept the little book, and learned the story.

And old John MacDougall told me the local minister told this story to John's grandmother. That's how he came to know it. So I'm telling it to you, and that's how you've come to know it.

Seal Mother

My father's two sisters Rachel and Nellie stayed in a camp, a large traveller-made tent, near Tarbert on Loch Fyneside in a wee field surrounded by rhododendron by the sea. When my Aunt Rachel told me this silkie tale I think I would have been fourteen, shortly after I'd left school. It was a summer's evening, so we were sitting inside the tent. And that's what Aunt Rachel always used to do in the evening – comb her hair. She had the most beautiful hair, so long she could sit on it and the colour of new-cut corn, pure yellow. She wasn't very old at that time, about thirty-eight. She'd never married.

I said, 'Aunt Rachel, you've got beautiful hair, it's the most beautiful hair I ever saw in my life. My Aunt Nellie has lovely hair too, but hers is grey.'

So she turned round and said to me, 'Brother [she called all her nephews brother], I'll tell ye a wee story. This has got to do wi hair – seeing you brought up the subject.'

So I'm going to tell you this story the way my Aunt Rachel told it to me. I hope you'll like it.

Many years ago away in the West Coast there lived a widow-woman and she had two beautiful daughters. Their father had been a fisherman and was drowned in an accident at sea, and the widow reared these two girls by herself. One's name was June and the other's name was May, called after the months they were born. This widow was the nicest person that ever walked this earth. She was respected and loved by the people in the village; it was a small village away from the shore a wee bit. She stayed by the seaside in a cottage that had been owned by her husband's father long before her time. And her two daughters attended the village school. But there was nothing in the world the widow wouldn't do to help anybody out in any circumstances – nothing was too hard for her. The most amazing thing about her was her hair – even though she was up in her mid-fifties it was a mass of golden curls right down her back. Everyone admired it and said it was the most beautiful they had ever seen.

The oldest daughter, June, a year older than May, was just like her mother in every way. Quiet, kindly, good-hearted, she would help anybody out in any circumstances. She loved her mother and when asked to do something she never spoke a single word back. But as June was good, May was wicked. She would do nothing for her mother. May was even hated by her school mates. They were pleased when she came fourteen that she left the school. But both girls, one after the other, left the school and stayed with their mother.

At the front of the cottage on the shoreside where they lived was a small island, about five or six acres of rocks and stones. When the tide went out there was a small strand, a bay of sand you could walk over to the island. The bay was famed for its cockles, and round it the mother used to send the girls to gather the seafood they loved to eat. But whenever the girls went to the island all May wanted was to go and torment the wee animals. In the summer-time she would go where the gulls were laying on the shoreside, break their eggs and throw them in the water. And then when she came to a nest with wee baby gulls she would catch them, put them in the sea to see if they would swim – it was horrible – they were just newly out of their eggs! And June would come back complaining to her mother.

But her mother was such a kindly person she never took sides, never said a word, just, 'Leave May alone. Someday she'll repent for her wickedness, June, you watch my words.'

Now the mother was a great knitter, she earned her living making jerseys, sweaters and cardigans. If she felt sorry for somebody, though they only gave her half price for a sweater, she would give it to them. So she would sit by the fireside knitting day out and day in. But at night-time she used to sit and let June comb her hair, the most beautiful golden hair you ever saw in your life. June wasn't her favourite. She never made fish of one or flesh of the other. But May would never take a turn at combing her mother's hair. She could always find some devilment to do instead. And May was never scolded.

Then one day the mother said to June, 'The tide is out. Will ye go and gather Mummy some cockles? Ask May if she'll go along with ye.'

And June in her bare feet took the basket, said, 'May, Mummy says we must go and gather cockles.'

'Well, I'll come with you but I'm not going to help,' she said.

So away they went. The mother looked out, saw the girls going. June carried the basket and May just splashed her feet across the water, walked with her head in the air doing nothing! The mother shook her head and sat down, started knitting again. By the time she'd finished the two girls had come back, and June had a full basket of cockles. She placed it down beside her mother:

'Mummy! May has been horrible today, really horrible. She never helped me, Mummy, in no way. When she came to the beach she picked up cockles and smashed them against the stones. She tormented a poor starfish and with a stick poked holes in a jellyfish washed up by the tide. Then she pulled the legs off three or four crabs, Mother, and turned them on their backs for the sun to get them. Mother, I just can't go on any longer with this, you'll have to do something about her! I know she's my sister, but why can't she be like you and me? Why can't she love these little creatures?'

The mother said, 'June, it's about time that she was taught a lesson.' That's all she said.

So naturally they had their supper and sure enough June said, 'Mummy, I want to brush your hair.'

June started to brush her mummy's hair and May went out to the shed where they had some hens for eggs. She started poking the hens with sticks, pulling their feathers, aggravating them in the shed.

The mother turned to June, 'Where is May?'

'Oh, you know, Mother, where she'll be – out tormenting the hens again!'

'Well,' she said, 'June, I think the time has come . . .'

'But Mother, we don't want to hurt her in any way.'

'Oh no,' she said, 'I'll no hurt your sister, you believe it. Not in any way!'

It was about the middle of summer, the month of July. And there were great tides. Sometimes during these heavy tides the small island across from where they stayed got completely bare, except for a part at the end where it was deep and full of rocks. So this one morning May got up and saw the tide was out as far as she could see across the strand. She hurried, had her breakfast, ran out to the beach. Her mother and June watched.

'There she goes, Mother,' June said. 'That's her on her way again. There's many a crab will lose its legs and many a jellyfish will be full o' holes before night-time, Mother, before the tide comes in. Mother, I'm really sorry!'

'Never mind, June, you go and tidy up yer bedroom.' And June went away to do her mother's bidding.

When June had walked into her bedroom and closed the door, the mother went and took down her sealskin coat that always hung behind the door. She put the coat over her shoulders, put her arms in it and walked away along the beach. Now by this time May had landed on the island that was covered in rocks and stones. People could disappear on it, and there was a big beach. May walked along it.

The mother walked along the shore till she came to a part where it was so deep the tide never went out very far; it was a heap of large rocks. She went behind one, pulled her sealskin coat up round her neck, sat down and clapped her hands three times above the water. She waited a wee while. Then lo and behold up came a big grey seal right in front of her. It never did anything, just came in right to where she sat with her coat over her behind the rock.

She said, 'Will ye go and tell *Mother* that May is on the island again up to her devilment? And I want *her* to teach May a lesson she'll never forget.'

The seal never spoke, just within minutes disappeared in the water and was gone. The mother walked back to the cottage, took off the sealskin coat, hung it behind the door, sat down and picked up her knitting, smiling to herself.

Now May had been walking round the island. She had picked up a large piece of stick and was poking everything she could see, wee bleeding pappies (the sea anemones) and a jellyfish. She pulled the nippers off a crab and turned it

over for the sun to get, so it was lying kicking. She enjoyed
this. Then she walked further in the island to a little part
that was covered in seaweed and tangles coming through a
break in the rocks. Sitting there was a baby seal three or four
weeks old.

When she saw it she said, 'I'm going to have some fun!'

So she started poking the baby seal with her stick. It went
'hsst hsst' at her. Baby seals can't bark, they only hiss like a
serpent because they're too young to have any other kind of
voice.

When lo and behold right at her back this voice spoke to
her, 'You wicked girl, why do you do that?'

And May turned round, she looked. Standing close
up behind her was a tall old woman with a long fur coat,
black fur coat buttoned right up to the neck. Her feet were
in sandals and her hair was hanging down her back in two
plaits. The woman's face was as wrinkled as a piece of old
skin, but her two eyes were shining out brown as a berry!
May was surprised.

'Why do you torment the little creatures?' she said.

May said, 'It's nothing to do wi you, old woman. Where
do you come from? You don't come from here!'

'What do *you* want coming here?' the woman said. 'This is
my place, this is *our* island!' she said.

And May said, 'I play here.'

'Well,' she said, 'you're not playing here any longer.'

'You've nothing to do with it, I'll tell my mummy about
you. And where do you come from anyway?'

'I know your mummy,' she said, 'and I know your sister.
They are nice persons. But you are evil.'

'What do ye want from me?'

She said, 'I'm wanting nothing *from* you; I want *you*!'
And just like that, before May could move, the old woman

jumped forward and snapped her by the wrist. It felt like a band of steel going round her arm. She caught her, held her tight.

'Let me go, let me go, I'll tell my mother!'

She said, 'Don't worry about your mother. I know yer mother perfectly well, and yer sister. But you, you must come with me!'

May tried her best to get her arm out of the old woman's grasp, but she held her in a vice grip of steel, though never hurt her. May couldn't move. The more she pulled the worse it got.

'P-please,' she said, 'let me go! I want to go home. Where are ye taking me to?'

The old woman said, 'I want you to come and meet my children. How you've tortured little creatures on this island is terrible! You ought to feel ashamed of yersel.'

'I don't feel no shame, I feel nothing. They're just little sea people, they should be tormented.'

'Well,' the old woman said, 'you need to be tormented! You must come with me.'

She half carried, half dragged her. May was trying to pull back but she was led further and further into the island, over rocks and through seaweed right to the end, a place May had never seen before. They came to a large pool that was left by the tide and surrounded by rocks. May looked and was surprised: sitting round the pool were four little girls. They looked identical, you couldn't pick one from the other.

The old woman said, 'Look, I want ye to come and meet my children!'

'I don't want to see any children, I want to go home to my mother.'

'You're not going home to your mother no way – till you have learnt yer lesson.'

So the old woman led May forward. In one hand she carried a walking stick. But this was not a natural stick; it was made from a large dried tangle, one of the dulse tangles people gather to make perfume. By the other hand she led May closer to the pool where these four young girls were sitting, beautiful and identical to each other, about the same age as May.

May's pulling against the old woman trying her best to escape from the grasp, 'Please, let me go back to my mummy, my mummy!'

'Evil child, you can't go. You've got to come here and meet my children.' She forced her to sit at the side of the large pool, three or four feet deep and two or three yards across. 'Now,' she said, 'why couldn't you, May, be like your mother and your sister? You wouldnae need to be here today – to go in this pool!'

May said, 'You're not putting me in any pool!'

'Yes, you're going in this pool. Because I'm going to see that you suffer the same way you made the little creatures on this island suffer. These children of mine are going to do the same thing to you that you have done to all these little creatures.'

'Oh please, please, don't do that to me!'

'Well,' she said, 'you've done it to them. Why shouldn't it be done to you? First we're going to put you in the pool, then you're going to become a crab and these little girls are going to pull off yer legs, pull off yer nippers. And see how you feel!'

'Oh please,' said May, 'please, please not . . . I don't want to —'.

'Well, you did it to the crabs, didn't you? Then *you're* going to become a cockle, and this one girl is going to smash ye against a stone. See how you fell then! Then you're going to be a jellyfish, and this girl here is going to poke holes in *you* with a stick. See how you feel! Then you're going to become a starfish and this one here is going to chop off yer legs with a stone – the same as you did!'

'Oh please, please, old woman, I couldn't stand it! Please let me go back to my mother.'

'Now children,' she said to the young ones, 'are you ready?' But they never spoke, never said a word. 'I think we'll start.'

May went down on her knees. But the old woman held her. And May begged mercy, swore she would never again touch another creature in the sea if the old woman would let her go.

So the old woman said, 'Well, seeing that your mother is a kindly soul and your sister is the nicest creature that walks this earth and hurts nobody, I'll give you one more chance! *But you must pay for your wickedness.*'

'Please, let me go. I'll never be wicked again, I'll not even come to the island.'

'Oh,' the old woman said, 'ye can come to the island. Join your sister gathering cockles to your heart's content, but you must learn to be good, leave the little creatures on the island alone.'

May begged from her heart and the old woman finally relented. She turned round:

'All right, children, ye can be gone!'

And just like that the four little girls disappeared over behind a rock. May never saw what happened, but these four little girls turned into seals and swam away in the water. The old woman still held her by the wrist, walked her back to the bay.

'Now,' she said, 'May, I know yer mother,' and she smiled to herself. 'And I know yer sister. I'm giving you one more chance. But ye have to pay for what ye've done in the past. You go home to your mother right now. Never let me see you doing another bad thing on this island as long as you live!'

She let go her arm. And the old woman stood with her stick in the sand made of a hard black tangle.

May was glad to get free. She ran as fast as she could across the bay. But something in her mind told her to stop – she looked back in case the old woman was following her. The old woman was gone . . . there was not a soul in sight. May ran all the way with her bare feet, and when she landed in her mother's house she was exhausted. May was as white as a ghost, shaking and terrified. Her mother just sat knitting by the fireside and her sister June was sitting reading a book. May was in such a state she couldn't even talk.

The mother looked at her and just smiled, 'Well, May, where have you been?'

'I-I've b-been on the island, Mother, and I had a t-terrible experience. I had a terrible experience on the island.'

'Were ye up to yer old tricks again, May, hurting little creatures?'

'Yes, Mother, I-I was hurting little creatures, I was really. But I'll never hurt them again.'

Her mother said, 'Come down here beside me and tell me all about it.'

'But Mother, I'm too terrified . . . they wanted me to be a crab and they wanted me to be a jellyfish!'

But the mother never asked any questions, no way. She didn't even want to hear the story.

She said, 'June, bring your sister something to eat.'

'Mother,' May said, 'I can't eat, I can't eat, Mother. I just want to be beside you, Mother. I feel terrible, I feel awful.'

And then May stepped by her mother. Behind where her mother was sitting knitting was a big wardrobe and on it was a large mirror. May looked in the mirror – to her horror her beautiful hair which had been like her mother's and like her sister June's was turned snow-white – as grey as grey could be, like a sheep!

She started to scream, 'Mummy, Mummy, Mummy, look at me, Mummy, look at me!'

Her mother turned round to her, 'What's the matter with you, May? You look all right to me.'

'Mother, Mother! Look at my hair, look, my hair is grey. It's grey!'

And her mother smiled again, said, 'Come here, May, and sit on my knee.' She put May on her knee and May was shaking with the fright, terrified.

'Mummy, Mummy, my beautiful hair is gone. My hair – it's grey. I could never survive like this, Mummy. What can I do?'

'Well, you would neither listen to me nor listen to your sister. You're only getting paid for your evil towards the little creatures on the island.'

'But Mummy, I can't go round the world with my hair . . . I'm like an old woman!'

She said, 'May, come closer and I'll tell ye a story.' May cuddled in and sat shaking on her mother's knee. She said, 'May, I had the same experience as you a long time ago. I was wicked just like you.'

'But Mother, your hair is beautiful, your hair is lovely, Mother!'

'But dearie,' she said, 'my hair wasn't as nice a long time ago as it is now. My hair was grey too when I was young, because I was wicked. And as time passed by and I changed my ways, my hair began to change. So now you've learned yer lesson. Sit here on your mummy's knee and from now on forget about being wicked! And prob'ly when ye start being good and change for the best then your hair'll come in as beautiful as mine; for everybody in the village wonders why a woman like me should have such beautiful hair.'

May began to get settled by this time. 'Is that true, Mother, is that true? Will the old woman never come back?'

'No, my dear,' she said, 'the old woman will never bother you any more, as long as you be kind and forget all your badness, stop torturing the little creatures on the island.'

'Mummy, Mummy,' she said, 'I'll never again do another evil thing.'

And sure to her word from that day on she never did an evil thing. May helped her mother in every way in the world. Her mother just needed to speak to her once. She came to her mother and asked to do good things. She walked to the village for her mother, and was kind and nice to all the people she met. But her grey hair remained.

Then one day her mother said to June, 'I think we'll have a meal of cockles today.'

And June said, 'Yes, Mother, I'll get the cockles.'

And May said, 'Mother, yes, I would like to go along and help!'

So their mother smiled. 'Well, girls,' she said, 'I'll finish off my little bit o' knitting if youse go and gather some for supper.'

So the two girls took the basket between them, a hand on each side and walked across the bay. The window of the house was facing the bay and the mother looked out. She saw the two girls walking, picking up the cockles together.

She smiled and said to herself, 'At last May has learned her lesson. Her hair'll not be grey for long, in another two or three months it'll be as good as ever, just like mine.' The mother stood looking out the window and smiled to herself.

Then knowing there was nobody in the house to hear, she turned round and said out loud, *'Isn't it nice when ye have silkies for friends!'*

And that's the end of my story.

Fair Maid's Tresses

When I left home at thirteen years of age I spent more time along the Hebrides. Now if you were to spend some time on the West Coast and the Hebrides, Islay and Jura, Tiree and Barra; well, there's a lot of edible seaweed along the West Coast of Scotland, dulse, and people go crazy for that kind of stuff. Sea lettuce it's called. There's two different kinds, the brown and the blue. But there's another kind of dulse that people wouldn't eat, it's known as 'Fair Maid's Tresses'. Now you know, fair maid's tresses is edible, but getting anybody to eat it would be a problem. Because it's only found in one particular area, one place in the world, and that's around the shores of Barra.

There's a great legend attached to the Fair Maid's Tresses a long time ago, and I'm about to tell you what took place.

You see, there're not many cliffs in Barra, well, some parts are kind o' clifty in Barra, but it's well away from Castlebay.

Along the coast in Castlebay there lived two sisters with their mother. They were beautiful young ladies, handsome. One was as dark as a raven and the other was as fair as could be, long golden hair, beautiful brown eyes. They were as far apart from each other as sisters could be, but they were full sisters. Their father was a fisherman, their father was lost at sea during a tragedy. They were brought up by their mother.

But the problem was, both of them were in love with the same young fisherman! And that young fisherman spent a lot of his time at sea. But he was in love with the blonde, the fair girl he adored. Every little chance he had he would come and spend the time with her. The old mother really adored the young fisherman. And the dark girl who was a year younger than her sister was madly in love with him. He treated her respectfully, but he didn't have the same time for her as he had for her sister. And the more attention he paid to her sister the more jealous she got. She was crazy with jealousy! Till one beautiful summer's morning.

She walks down to the old wise woman in the village who lived alone, and she says to the old wise woman:

'I want you to teach me a song, an enchanting song!'

She says, 'What do you mean, girl?'

'I want you to teach me a song that will enchant anyone I sing it to.'

And she persuaded the old wise woman in the village, an old herbalist, what we would call today a henwife in the stories. But she persuaded the old wise woman to teach her an enchanting song in Gaelic, a Gaelic enchanting song. Whoever heard it would reminisce in their mind and fall asleep. And she taught her over and over again every evening till she had it complete.

And then one day, it was a beautiful sunny morning. The raven-haired girl asked her sister would she like to come for a walk. Sister was overjoyed; her young boyfriend was away at sea. She took her sister away along the coast of Barra by Castlebay, not to the beaches but to the rough rocks. And the tide was full out.

She and her sister walked down. They sat down on a rock well out on the tide shore, cliffs behind them. And she took a brush with her, a hair brush:

'Sister,' she says, 'I want to comb your hair!'

She began to brush her sister's golden locks that came down near her knees when they were brushed. And as she brushed her sister's golden hair she sang the song from the old wise woman, the Gaelic song, the enchanting song. Soon she saw her sister's eyes close, and her sister fall asleep.

While her sister was asleep she kept on singing and she weaved her sister's hair into the seaweed, the local seaweed on the rocks, the rough coarse seaweed. She wove her sister's hair, every single part of her sister's hair into the rocks on the seaweed while her sister lay asleep on the warm rocks in the sunshine.

Meanwhile the tide was coming in, the tide was coming in gradually. Every single strand of her sister's hair was woven into the seaweed, and she waited till the tide was lapping around her sister's feet. Her sister was still asleep, enchanted with the songs of Gaelic. And the tide got closer.

She ran up to the rocks above and watched the tide coming in. She watched the tide come up to her sister's legs, she watched the tide come up to her sister's waist as she sat on the rocks above. She watched the tide come up to her sister's breasts, up to her sister's neck and just as the tide was coming up to her sister's head she saw a strange thing: she saw a big grey seal swimming as fast as it could. As the water lapped over her sister's head the seal dived down beside her sister!

She ran to the cliffs above and watched . . . for a little moment there was silence. And then she saw *two seals* come up from where her sister would have been. They looked at her on the rocks and swam away out into the bay. She was so angry and so upset she tried to call out, but no sound came from her voice. And she threw herself over the cliff into the sea!

But the wind caught her cape and spread her cape out and she floated . . . as she floated she became a *cormorant*, a black ugly bird of the sea and landed in the water still crying to her sister:

'I'm sorry, I'm sorry, I'm sorry!'

But the two seals were gone.

So came the legend of the cormorant. And today that's why if you see a seal it always snaps at the cormorant. Some people say it's because cormorants steal a lot of fish and the seals don't like them. But seals and cormorants don't get on together. If a seal comes swimming along and there's a cormorant in his way, he'll make a snap at it to get it out of its way. But it's not because cormorants steal a lot of fish; it's because the cormorant tried to steal the young seal man's wife a long time ago.

That's the legend of the story. And today, if you walk the beaches in Barra you will see beautiful seaweed, edible seaweed, that's known as Fair Maid's Tresses. But no one in Barra will eat it, because of the story that's told.

Seal Island

I find great pleasure in telling seal stories because they meant a lot to the people of the Hebrides and the Western Isles. They took these stories to heart. Stories that have never been published or written down in any form; I collected them. I grew up by the seals, I slept with the seals . . . that was a strange story I would like to tell you.

There was a little island when I was a kid, nearby where I lived. And of course one day I was sitting in school I was so hungry, I couldn't listen to the teacher because I had no breakfast, no food at home or nothing. I asked to leave the room. And there was an old man Campbell, he had a bad eye. He always sat in the summer seat. So instead of going to the toilet, as I had asked to leave the room to go to the toilet, I walked down to the old man where he sat on the shoreside. I can visualize it just like yesterday and that's over sixty-five years ago.

And I said to him, 'Donald can you give me a couple of matches?'

'Of course,' he said, 'boy, I'll give you a couple of matches,' and he gave me a couple.

I walked the bay out to the little island. And I had a little billy can, just a jam tin with a piece of wire in it; I had done this before. Now I had to walk maybe half a mile. The tide was out, the strand was bare. The little island was bare; there was nothing on it, a few bushes, grass, no trees. I filled the tin full of whelks and mussels and limpets and cockles, and I kindled a little fire of driftwood, held them with a stick to boil. I can just visualize it just like yesterday and this is true. Sure it doesn't take long to boil! I boiled it a couple of times and I took them, poured the water off. I'm sitting there eating the limpets, eating the mussels and clabbidhus that I put in the skillet; felt better, felt my stomach getting full up.

But I didn't realise while I was sitting enjoying myself with the little fire – the tide was coming in. And these tides rush very quickly. Before I realized, I'd spent nearly two hours there on the little island. And I could swim a wee bit but I couldna swim all that distance – the tide was full in! I was trapped like Robinson Crusoe on the little island by myself. I could see the village in the distance across. I had nothing to fear.

So I said, 'There's only one thing for it,' I just had to stay there.

And I was all right. I wasnae hungry. There was nae water because there's nae water on the wee island. But I made a wee bed to myself under the bushes and gathered all the dry grasses and gathered bits of driftwood, had my fire. And the day passed very quickly. The tide was still in. And then, in the evening I made my wee bed, lay down and kept myself warm, happed myself up the best way I could.

Then they started coming in, the seals! They came in, and they came in and they came in – this was their resting place for the night. I'm lying there – just as close as that settee is to you, Linda! There lying beside me was a big bull seal, a big one.

And he groaned all night long 'uhhung, oongh, oongh'.

And I said, 'Will you shut up for a while and give me peace to sleep!'

But he paid no attention to me. The other seals they were quiet, young ones. They're lying all scattered across, maybe about, not a lot but we may say about a dozen.

I must have fell asleep, because when I woke in the morning the sun was shining, all the seals were gone and the tide was full out. And I felt a bit hungry. I knew what I was going to do when I walked back.

I gathered a bundle of driftwood and took it to an old woman in the village. She always gave me a sixpence and a piece and jam for my bundle of driftwood I'd gathered. And sixpence then was a lot of money.

So I don't know; they probably sent the older boys down to look for me, my parents said, but they couldn't find me anyhow. Nobody knew what had happened. But they never reported me to the police or anything. They knew some nights we stayed out all night long. It was the natural thing.

But it was years later when I left home about thirteen that I was working with an old fisherman down near Carradale. After visiting my Aunt Rachel in Tarbert I went down to Carradale, looking for a wee bit of work. I was thirteen, able to look after myself! And I got a job to help him to mend his nets. I was good at mending nets, taking seaweed and things out of the nets, helping him to clean the net and maybe get half a crown for fags. I told him about this carry on on the island same as I'm telling you. And then I found something I'd never known:

He said, 'Duncan, you know what was wrong with the old fellow?'

I said, 'No!'

'Well,' he said, 'he wouldna hurt you.'

'Oh no, no,' I says, 'he wouldna hurt me in any way.'

He said, 'He was suffering from the toothache! With the wet fish in their mouth, you know, and eating the wet fish their poor teeth gets rotten and they have to suffer till they fall out. They can't go to a dentist here, poor creatures! You should have felt sorry for him instead of shouting at him.'

And that's a true story.

Jack and the Golden Peats

Jack lived with his father and mother a long time ago in Ireland. They had a small croft. Jack's father cut peats for a living; he had a wonderful peat bank. But Jack's father, like many others, was very fond of the drink. And by drinking too much he couldn't go to his work. Things went from bad to worse and finally he had to sell his peat bank to someone else. Oh, he was heartbroken when he had to sell it, for he had a young son and a wife to take care of. But anyhow, his wife was a wee bit cleverer than him; and by running the small croft herself – she had a few ducks and a few hens – she managed to survive and keep them in a little bit of food. But this worried the old man because he had nothing to do. From bad to worse, he got worse and worse on the drink. After a few years he finally died. And by this time Jack was ten years old.

So, Jack and his mother spent the next years by themselves. But Jack had a burning ambition; he wanted to be a peat cutter like his father. He wanted to own a peat bank, the best one in Ireland.

When he came fifteen years old he said, 'Mother, I'll have to get a job.'

'Well, son,' she says, 'for God's sake don't be like your father! Don't go peat cutting, because you'll never amount to anything.'

'But, Mother, it's in my blood. There's nothing I want to do, than cut peats.'

'Well, son, you'll never do any better than your father'd done unless you get a real peat bank to yourself. And there's no way in the world we can afford to buy one because a peat bank costs a lot of money.'

'Well, Mother,' he said, 'maybe if I got a job and worked for someone, maybe through the years I could get my own peat bank.' It was a large lump of moor, you see, and you had to be a landowner to own a peat bank.

But anyway, Jack went off one morning and he wandered far and wide across the moors looking for a job, asking peat cutters, to help them lift the peats or set them up to dry. But everybody said they couldn't afford to give anybody any work. But he crossed over this hill where he'd never been before in his life, and he saw a large moor. He could see peats up drying, a peat stack. And he came down through the moor and there he came to an old man working by himself. When he came down the old man was very pleasant.

'Well, young fellow,' he said, 'where are you going to?'

Jack said, 'I'm looking for work.'

'Work,' he said 'I have plenty!'

'Well,' Jack said, 'I'm willing to work if you've got any for me.'

'I'm just about to have a wee bit of lunch,' he said, 'a sandwich. Would you like to join me?'

And Jack sat down beside this old man . . . he looked kind of queer, more like an elf or a fairy or a goblin or something than he actually looked like a man. He had big ears, a long nose and a long chin. Jack could see he was a human being, not a fairy or a goblin or anything; but Jack had never seen a queerer looking old person in his life.

He said, 'Where do you come from, my son?' So Jack told him. 'Oh,' he said, 'your mother'll be Mary!'

'Mary – that's my mother's name,' said Jack.

'Well,' he said, 'to tell you the truth, son, I knew your mother a long time ago. In fact, me and your mother . . . I'm not going to say the word . . . were lovers.'

'Well,' Jack said, 'I know nothing about this.'

He said, 'I've never seen your mother for years. And they tell me your father has died.'

Jack said, 'My father is dead, died five years ago. And I'm looking for a wee job to get myself a bit of a peat bank.'

'Well, I can remember your father. In fact, he beat me to your mother!'

'Well,' Jack said, 'that's no business o' mine!'

'Anyhow, if you're willing to work with me I'll give you a job. But look, I'll tell you something; as you walk home tonight I'll accompany you to the village after we're finished working.'

So, they sat down and had a sandwich together. They worked all day and the old fellow was a good peat cutter. He could cut peats like no one on this earth; he was throwing them up and Jack was setting them up in threes to dry.

After they worked hard, it was just about evening time, he said, 'Son, I think we'll stop. Now I'll walk you home, I would love to see your mother.'

'Well,' Jack said, 'if you walk to the village you should stop by for a cup of tea.'

So, the two of them packed up their materials for the night and put all their cutting stuff into a wee shed. Then the old man went to this little shed, took out a strange kind of long coat that came to his heels, not waterproof, more like skin. Jack had never seen anything like this before in his life. And the old man put it on.

He said, 'Come on, my son, we'll go and see your mother.'

So, the two of them walked home and came to the wee croft where Jack's mother stayed. And Jack explained about the old man.

The old woman looked; she said, 'Michael!'

'Mary!' he said, and they shook hands with each other.

She says, 'Come in, the kettle's just boiling.' So she welcomed Michael into the house.

'Well, Mother,' Jack said, 'I know all about you – he explained to me!' So they sat and talked and had tea.

Michael said, 'That's a fine young son you have, Mary.'

'Oh well,' she said, 'he's growing up to be a nice young man.'

'Well, to tell you the truth,' he said, 'he tells me he's looking for a peat bank.'

'Ach,' she said, 'he'll never afford a peat bank.'

'Well,' he says, 'I'm getting kind of old and I think I've had my time. In fact, I think, I was making up my mind to go on a journey for a while. I think that, I've taken a notion to your son Jack – I'm going to turn over my peat bank to Jack lock, stock and barrel!'

'Ah, but you can't do that!' she says. 'What will you do for yourself?'

'Oh,' he said, 'I'll no need it, Mary. I've enough to keep me going. You remember, I still stay by the smiddie, by the old smiddie house in the village. And if ever you and Jack are in the village, come and give me a visit!'

And he took a big paper from his pocket with his name 'Michael' on it, and he signed his whole peat bank over to Jack. He shook hands with Mary and shook hands with Jack, and then he was gone.

'Mother,' he says, 'what kind of man is that?'

'O Jack,' she said, 'it's a long story: long afore I met your father Michael and me was good friends. In fact, if it wasn't for your father . . .' and she began tidying her hair up a wee bit, you know, tidying her hair with her hand; 'Michael and me – Michael could have been your father!'

'Well, he's like a father to me,' he said. 'Did you see the peat bank he's gien me? Mother, there's thousands of pounds of peats there. It'll do me all my life.'

'Well, Jack,' she said, 'you're lucky.'

And so Jack got his first peat bank. Jack was overjoyed! He could cut peats, he could sell them and through time he would manage to buy himself a donkey and cart, he would work on his way. He had a peat bank for himself! But every morning bright and early Jack was up, off to his peat bank.

One morning he was working very hard when he heard a voice saying, 'Aha! Jack, you're busy!'

Didn't Jack think it was Michael coming back for a visit. And Jack looked round – behind him sat a wee man about two feet high with a wee spade beard and a wee black coat on him. Jack was mesmerized.

He said, 'Where do you come fae?'

'Oh never mind,' he said, 'Jack, where I come fae! I've come to see you.'

But Jack said, 'What do you want off me; do you want peats?'

'Oh no, Jack,' he said, 'I'm no wanting peats. I know about you, Jack, and I know how you got the peat bank from Michael. And I know about your mother. Jack, I know everything about you – I've chosen you.'

'*Chosen me,*' says Jack, 'what have you chosen me for? I'm busy working here.'

He said, 'Jack, I want you to do something for me.'

But Jack said, 'I cannae do nothing for you – I'm a peat cutter.'

'Jack,' he said, 'I can make that bank worth your while if you will do something for me.'

Jack said, 'What are you? Are you a leprechaun or something? You're nae bigger than one.'

'Well, we'll no say whether I am or no.' He never said he was or he wasn't; but he says, 'Jack, I want you to do something for me, and I'll make it worth your while.'

Jack said, 'What do you want me to do for you?'

He said, 'Jack, I want you to do something special for me,' and he crept with his wee short legs up to the top of where Jack had set the last three peats. They set the peats in threes to get them dry. And he picked up a peat, lifted it, 'Jack, they're good peats. You're a good cutter and you're learning well. Jack, do you think you could make me a sword from a peat?'

'Aye, now come!' says Jack, 'I'm a peat cutter! There's naebody could make a sword from a peat.'

'Aye, Jack,' he says, 'I want you to have me a sword made from a peat.'

Jack said, 'There's naebody under the sun could make a sword from a peat.'

'Aye, Jack, *you* could! I want you to take a peat to the village; I want you to go to the blacksmith's shop no far from old Michael's house. And I want you to have a sword made from a peat, and meet me here tomorrow night. Jack, I'll make it worth your while. Dinnae you worry about cutting peats!'

But Jack said, 'There's naebody in the world can make a sword from a peat!'

He says, 'Come here a minute, Jack! *Lift that peat!*'

Jack lifted the peat. Now, a peat itself when it's dry is about a pound and a half. Jack tried to lift the peat. The peat was about twenty or thirty pounds in weight! But it wasn't a peat, not a common peat; it was pure gold, a golden peat!

Jack said, 'That's no a peat!'

'No,' the wee man said, 'that's no a peat, Jack. It has the name of a peat, Jack, but it's a *golden peat*. And what I want you to do for me, Jack, is take this peat to the blacksmith. You know the blacksmith well; he knows Michael, he knows your mother. And tell him he must keep his mouth shut and not say a word. But he must make me a sword out of this peat, a golden sword! And you must meet me here tomorrow night with the sword. And tell him whatever's left over from the peat he can keep it to himself.'

Oh, Jack was overjoyed, over the moon this had ever happened to him – first body in Ireland to have a golden peat!

'Now, Jack,' he says, 'go home, have your tea with your mother. And take my peat o the smiddie and get me a sword! I'll tell you what I want you to do later. Now remember, Jack, it's worth your while.' The wee man was gone.

Jack sat there dumbfounded, scratching his hair. There before him lay a golden peat that would buy half of Ireland – a golden peat eight inches long, six inches broad, solid gold weighing nearly thirty pounds.

Jack said, 'In the name of God, what am I going to do with this?' He could barely lift it. But he knew in his mind, in his heart if this wee man could turn one peat into gold, he could turn in many, many more.

So he carried it back under his arm, took it home – took him barely to carry it back to his mother. And he walked into the house, put it on the table.

His mother says, 'Jack, what's that, laddie, what's that you've got?' So, Jack told his mother the story.

She says, 'Jack, that's a leprechaun. And, son, never fall foul of a leprechaun in the world! What does he want you to do?'

'Mother,' he said, 'he wants me to make him a sword in the blacksmith's shop.'

'Oh,' she says, 'Jack, Jack, you know what you've got your hands on, Jack – that's more gold than all that's in Ireland! Look, Jack, you listen to your mother, forget about cutting peats. You do what the wee man tells you, and I'm sure you'll come off all right. You go to the blacksmith; I know him well. The smiddie's house is just . . .'

'I ken, Mother, I've passed it many times,' says Jack.

She says, 'It's no far from Michael's house, and you'll probably see Michael when you're there.'

The next morning after breakfast Jack takes the peat below his oxter – he could barely carry it – and he walks to the village. It wasn't far, maybe a mile. And he goes to the old blacksmith. The blacksmith is busy shoeing a donkey. Jack comes in. He has the peat wrapped in a bag so's nobody will see it. He waits till the old fat blacksmith has shod the donkey for the man who owned it.

'And hello, Jack!' the blacksmith said, 'what can I do for you?'

'Blacksmith,' he said, 'I've a wee job for you.'

'Oh aye, Jack, I haena seen you for a while. What are you busy at, Jack?'

Jack told him, 'I'm busy cutting peats.'

'Oh aye,' he says.

So, Jack took the bag off the peat and put it on the top of the anvil. The old blacksmith's eyes lighted up:

'Laddie, laddie, what's that you've got?'

Jack says, 'A peat.'

He said, 'Laddie, that's no a peat; that's gold!'

Jack said, 'I ken it's gold.'

'Where in the world did you ever get that?' he says.

'Never mind where I got it. But I want you to do something for me!'

'O Jack!' he said, 'I'll do anything for you; laddie, do you know what you've got? That could buy half of Ireland!'

'Never mind!' says Jack. 'Look, are you busy?'

'Well, no really, I'm no very busy.'

He said, 'Do you think you could make me a sword out of that, a good sharp sword?'

'Aye,' says the blacksmith, 'I believe I could. Gold's easy to work with, Jack, it doesna need het very much. I could maybe chop you a blade out of that.'

'Well, 'Jack said, 'look, you make me a blade out of that, a good hand sword, and whatever's left ower you can keep it to yourself!'

Oh, the old blacksmith rubbed his hands in glee, 'Jack, I'll make you a sword, laddie; I'll make you the best golden sword in Ireland!'

Jack said, 'Listen, you've to tell nobody! Whatever's left over abien, you keep it to yourself. But you must never mention a word about this.'

'I promise, Jack,' he said, 'I won't say a word!'

'All right,' says Jack, 'you carry on making the sword. I'm going to see my old friend, old Michael. I'll be back in a wee while.'

Jack left the smiddie and walked up to Michael's house, a wee thatched house covered with ivy and honeysuckle. The curtains were drawn, the back door locked and the front door locked. He knocked in the front and in the back, and looked in the window. But old Michael was gone. Jack went round the house three times shouting his name, but old Michael wasn't there.

Jack said to himself, 'I wonder where he went to; he said he was going on a journey, he must have gone off.'

So, Jack went back down to the smiddie and stood. By this time the old blacksmith was chopping out a blade, the most beautiful long golden blade with a handle on it. And he took a big file, sharpened it each side. And he made a sword to Jack about two feet long – chopped out of solid gold.

'There you are, Jack,' he says, 'but what do you want it for?'

'I don't know what I want it for; I can't even tell you.' And there was a heap of clippings, all the wee pieces of gold he was not using. Jack says, 'Look, keep this to yourself – but don't mention it to a soul!'

The old blacksmith says, 'Look, I'm closing shop, closing! I've never had as much in my life; this'll do me from now on – no more blacksmith for me!'

So, Jack bade the old blacksmith farewell and away Jack went with the golden sword in his hand. Back he went to his mother. He showed it to her and held it up. It was fairly glittering in the light of the lamp inside the wee house.

'Jack,' she says, 'that's a bonnie thing, laddie, a bonnie thing!'

'Aye, Mother, but I wonder what the wee man wants with it.'

'O laddie, I tellt you before and I'll tell you again, never fall foul of a leprechaun! Jack, it is a leprechaun.'

'Well, Mother, leprechaun here or leprechaun there, I have to meet him tonight!'

So, back Jack goes to his peat bank. And when he came back to where he had begun to cut, there was the wee man sitting with his legs crossed once again.

'Aha, Jack!' he said, 'I see you're back! How did you get on?'

'I got on fine,' he said.

'Did you get my sword?' he asked.

'Oh, I got your sword,' and he held it up.

The wee man came up with his wee toy short legs. He wetted his thumb and tried one side, and he tried the other side.

He says, 'Jack, perfect – perfect, my son, perfect!'

'There,' Jack said, 'it's yours!'

'Oh no, Jack,' he said, 'it's no mine; it's yours!'

'But,' Jack said, 'what am I going to do with it? I've no need for it.'

'Oh aye, Jack, you've need for it all right, you've need for it! Do you ken that clifts in the back of your mother's house?' Now, at the back of Jack's mother's house were the cliffs as big as what you see there, the Cuillins of Skye, great big rocks in the hillside.

'Aye,' Jack said, 'I ken them well; I used to play on them when I was a laddie.'

He said to Jack, 'Tonight at twelve o'clock you'll come up there and bring your sword with you. When you come to the clift you'll see an opening and you'll see a light.'

Jack said, 'There's nae opening in the clift there.'

'Oh aye, Jack,' he said, 'there is – and I'll be waiting for you! Now promise me you'll be there when the clock strikes twelve.'

Jack said, 'Oh well, if that's what you want.'

And the wee man was gone. Jack couldn't work that evening he was so excited. He went home to his mother and told her.

'Oh well, Jack,' she said, 'I dinnae ken, laddie, whether it's enchantment or what it is. But laddie, I'll tell you one thing, you're better to do what the wee man tells you because if you fall foul of a leprechaun your life will never be the same again! If I was you I would carry on, just do what he's telling you, because it might be lucky for you.'

So, to make a long story short, that night after Jack had a sip of tea with his mother, he couldn't wait to see what was going to happen. He wanted to see the whole story through! He hadn't far to go, about half a mile from the back of his mother's house. And he walked up to the cliff face just before twelve o'clock. When he came to the great big high rocks he saw flashes, and flashes, flashes of light, lights flashing!

'This must be the place,' says Jack to himself.

So, he has the sword under his oxter and he walks up. Sure enough there was a large opening in the cliff face, and there was the wee man.

'Welcome, Jack,' he said, 'I was waiting on you. In you come!'

And Jack walked in. The whole place was lighted up. There was a great chamber, a big monster room and a big space on the floor made of solid rock. There was a big stone chair in the middle of the floor. And as Jack came in with the wee man the light got brighter, and he saw the rock behind closing behind him.

Jack thought to himself, 'What's happening here?' But he wasn't afraid of the wee man.

The man says, 'Jack, just in a few minutes you'll be all right . . . just in a few minutes, all right! The dancing will start.'

Jack said, 'What in the world am I doing here, in the name of God?'

And he still had his sword. Then the music started and within minutes hundreds and hundreds of little people came out to the floor. They all stood in rows. Then a wee man a bit bigger than the leprechaun that Jack had dealt with to make the golden sword came out; he had a crown on his head. He came up.

'Hie! Jack, my laddie,' he said, 'you've come at last! We were waiting for you – you're the very man!' And he shook hands with him. 'Now, Jack,' he said, 'listen to me: there's only one job I have for you, my laddie, and I'm glad you've come here. We're going to make it worth your while! Pay nae attention to the dancing. Pay nae attention to anything else, *but hang your hands on to that sword* – for grim death and don't let it go – because, laddie, you're going to need it!'

Jack was mesmerized. What was happening here? Where was he? He was in a strange land among strange folk, strange people. But then the music got louder and louder. All the women started to dance. And the king sat on his stone chair.

Then they started to scream and run for their lives – out from behind the rocks came a great monster snake with two heads on it. Up it came over the top of the rock by the king's chair, and the wee king's running below his chair.

'Now, Jack,' he says, '*use your sword*!'

And Jack ran over – snap-snap, off with the two heads of the big snake. In a minute, there it lay – two heads cut clean through.

And the wee king came up, shook hands with Jack:

'Jack, my laddie, you've done it! You ken, we've been tortured, laddie, for hundreds of years with that beast, and there was nobody could save us but a human being with a golden sword. Now you've done it! And Jack, whatever you want you can have it.'

Then up comes the leprechaun: 'Jack,' he says, 'look over there!'

And Jack looked. There was a peat stack, but it wasn't peats; it was golden peats. And at the side of the heap of peats was a wheelbarrow, a peat barrow.

The king shook hands with Jack. He says, 'Jack, my son, we'll never see you again. But look, you've got two minutes, two minutes only to get that barrow and fill it with as much as you can take!'

Then the rock began to open.

He says, 'Jack, you've only two minutes to get through that opening!'

And Jack rushed over.

'Go on,' says the wee leprechaun, 'help yourself! Get as many as you can on that barrow and get through that opening. If you don't in two minutes, you'll never see the outside world again!'

Jack rushed to the peat barrow. He put as many golden peats packed in as he could. And he whirled trying to get through the opening. But just as the rock was closing the barrow cowped, fell and spilled. Jack grabbed one peat and went out through the opening. The rock door closed behind him and he stood there mesmerized, rubbing his hair.

'God Almighty,' he said, 'what's happened to me? Where have I been?'

And he looked: he had one golden peat below his oxter and the rock face was solid. He walked home with the peat under his oxter to his mother. He put it on the table.

She says, 'Jack, Jack, how did you get on?'

'Well, Mother, dinnae speak to me, you've never been through what I've been through!' He placed it further in on the table.

She says, 'Jack, that's solid gold, laddie – that can buy all the peat banks in Ireland.'

Jack said, 'I ken that!'

And Jack sold his golden peat, he sold his peat bank and bought himself a big rich farm. Jack became one of the richest men in Ireland.

And that's the last of my story.

'Jack and the Golden Peats' was told to me by an old Irishman a long time ago when I worked in the Shirra Glen, when they were building the Loch Floy Dam. They said that was a true story that happened in Ireland a long time ago . . . well, if all stories are true, that's no lie!

John Broom

There once lived two old sisters. Their mother and father had died when the sisters were very young, in their teens, and they'd been left with a small farm. The sisters stayed by themselves, none of the two of them had ever married. One was a couple of years older than the other. And they kept some cows, hens and sheep and some small cattle in their farm. They lived very happy. But the funny thing was – they didn't have much land for ploughing or anything, it was mostly grass in their place – but the place was nearly covered in broom.

All these broom bushes grew around the farm. And it didn't matter how often they got some men out from the village to cut them, make places for their cattle and sheep and goats to feed from the grass, the broom always came back. If they neglected it for two or three years, the place was nearly buried in broom! But things didn't always work out as well as possible for the two old sisters . . . things seemed to go from bad to worse.

The broom began to crawl up round the farm and grow stronger and bigger every year. The hens stopped laying one day, then the cows went dry and the sheep took sick. The one man who used to work for the sisters had to be paid off because they couldn't afford to keep him working. Things really got difficult!

And one day they had nothing left on the farm but some oatmeal – they had no eggs, no milk, no nothing. So the younger sister said to the older:

'Look, Sister, we will have to make something for breakfast.'

She said, 'Sister, we have very little for breakfast this morning. We have some oatmeal to make some porridge, but we don't even have a fire to cook it on.'

'Well,' the younger one said, 'that should be easy. Wait a minute and I'll go out and get some broom. There is lots of it around the farm. I'll gather some roots of rotten broom and we'll soon have a good fire going. We'll put on a pot of porridge and you and I will have a breakfast. It's not much, but it is better than nothing!'

So she quickly put on her apron and wandered out. She was gathering roots of broom where the old bushes had died out and putting them in her apron. She went down behind this one broom bush and lying beside it was a wee baby – the bonniest wee boy she had ever seen in her life – about a year old! He was lying on his back beside the bush giggling and laughing and clapping his hands.

And the old woman was so excited, so amazed she didn't know what to do. She picked him up, put him on the top of the broom in her apron and hurried back as quickly as she could. She rushed in the door and was out of breath when she landed in.

She said, 'Sister, sister!'

And her sister said, 'What is it?'

'Look! Look what I've found!'

And her sister said, 'What is it? Is it some eggs or something you found among the broom that the hens have been laying and that we knew nothing about?'

'No, it is not eggs, it is something better than eggs!'

'What is it then?' and she ran into the kitchen.

'It is a baby boy!'

And her sister came and said, 'A baby boy! How in the name of heaven could a baby boy get here?'

And she looked and saw the baby, took him off her sister's apron, took him in her arms and cuddled him. He started to smile at her.

'Oh dear-dearie me!' she said. 'Where do you come from, little man?'

And her sister said quickly, 'He is probably hungry – kindle up the fire and make the porridge – but don't make it too thick! And I'll feed him some. We'll keep him and nobody will ever know we have him – he was sent to us and we'll keep him!' They kindled up the fire and made porridge, but they fed the baby first.

So they sat and the two of them were so excited they forgot all their worries, they forgot about everything else but this baby. And one wanted to hold him in her lap, then the other one wanted to. And they went upstairs, collected all the blankets and all the old sheets they could find.

One said they were going to make clothes for him: 'We'll do everything for him and . . . where could he sleep?'

'Oh!' said the older sister, 'my granny's cradle is still up the stair.'

She ran up, got the cradle and brought it down. She scrubbed it, washed it and filled it full of nice clean woollen blankets and put the baby in it.

But the funny thing about this wee baby was that it never cried; he just lay giggling in the cradle! And both of them loved him.

But shortly after they had fed the baby and fed themselves

some porridge, they were sitting discussing what they were going to call him.

'We must give him a name,' one of the sisters said. 'We will call him Alex.'

'No, we'll not call him Alex,' said the other. 'We will call him something else . . . we will call him Archie.'

'No, we'll not call him Archie,' said the younger sister who'd found him. 'I know what we will call him, we'll call him *John Broom*.'

And both of them said, 'That's a lovely name! We'll just call him John Broom.'

And John Broom he was. Both were discussing the name when the sun glistened, the cockerel started to crow and the hens started to cackle. And the sisters said:

'Listen, listen to the hens and listen to the cockerel! That's never happened for months.'

So the younger sister walked out to see what was happening: all the hens were making such an excitement and carrying on, and the cockerel was on top of the rafters. He was crowing away and the hens were all cackling.

She said, 'These hens must be laying,' and she walked into the hen-shed.

Sure enough, every nest in the shed was full of eggs. They kept a lot of hens, about three or four dozen, and every nest was full – more eggs than they could ever use!

Then she listened: the cow in the byre said 'moo-moo' and started to carry on its noise. And round she went to the byre, there was the cow and standing by its side was a wee baby calf – the cow had calved!

She ran back as fast as she could. She said, 'Sister, sister, come quick till you see this! The cow has calved and the hens have started to lay!'

'Oh dear me,' said her sister, 'what has happened to the place?'

So they ran out. There was the baby calf and there were the hens.

'Now,' she said, 'we have milk and eggs and John Broom will have plenty to eat!'

So they started drinking milk. And eggs – they had so many eggs that they had to take some to the village the next day. And the next day the egg boxes were full again. They had so much milk that they could hardly use it all, so they had to start selling it in the village.

Next day another cow calved and the same thing happened again, they had to sell more milk. And John Broom was getting bigger, the days passed on. They made him clothes. They got so many eggs and so much milk sold every day in the village that the old women began to get rich. From the day John Broom came they never looked back.

They employed a man from the village now they had some money to come and cut the broom, tend the fences and look after the sheep and milk the goats. They sold almost everything produced on the farm. Five or six years passed by.

John Broom began to grow up and run about. Ten years passed by, now John was ten. The old ladies loved him like he was their own wee son. And the funny thing was, nobody in the village ever even asked a question where he came from! John Broom grew up to be the most beautiful, sturdiest lad you ever saw. Another five years passed by and this day John was fifteen.

He called them aunties and was such a beautiful young man. The old ladies used to sleep upstairs and John Broom slept downstairs. He slept by the fire and he worked hard, he made that farm a different place all together. By this time the old ladies were rich, really rich.

One morning both of them came down for their breakfast. They looked at the side of the fire on John Broom's bed . . . but John Broom was gone, John Broom was gone! They searched around the farm, they shouted and they shouted, they searched every place. John Broom had disappeared as quickly as he had come. They were so upset and heartbroken they did not know what to do.

Then gradually as the days passed by things began to go bad again. Things got worse. In fact, the sisters never tended the cattle and they never tended the sheep. They sold the cows. The hens stopped laying. They sold all the sheep. And the broom began to creep up round the farm again. Five years passed by and by this time the two old sisters had spent every single penny keeping themselves alive.

They were sitting by the fire wondering what was going to happen, they didn't have any sticks, nothing – everything was as bad as the day John Broom came. And the funny thing was, they loved him and respected him, thought so much of him that one wouldn't mention his name to the other, even when they went to their bed at night and both of them slept in the one small room upstairs.

Then at five o'clock one morning the cock started to crow and wakened the old women up. The older sister said:

'Sister, listen! The cock is starting to crow, every cock in the place is starting to crow!'

Now they didn't have any cattle, they had sold everything off. But the cock had started at five o'clock in the morning and there was such a racket about the farm the old women were upset. They didn't know what was going on.

So the older sister, she got a lamp and came downstairs. And when she landed downstairs the fire was burning in the grate, a great fire burning in the grate! She looked over: there lying in his bed was John Broom – back again – he was once more in his bed! She never touched him, never said a word.

She ran back up the stairs and said to her sister, 'Sister, waken! Are you awake?'

And she said, 'What is it, what's all the trouble, what's all the carry-on?'

She said, 'I've something to tell you . . .'

'What is it? Tell me!'

'John is home!'

Her sister could hardly believe it. She couldn't sleep anymore. She got up, dressed herself and came down. Sure enough, John Broom was back in his bed, sound asleep.

And they walked quietly: 'Don't disturb him, let him sleep. You put on the porridge and make breakfast.'

And she put on a great pot of porridge, then wakened John Broom up. They gave him some breakfast. They never even asked him where he had been.

And the only thing was, he said: 'Aunties . . .'

'What is it,' they said, 'John?'

'Why did you give me the porridge without any milk? You never do that, give me porridge without any milk in the morning for my breakfast, Auntie!'

She said, 'John, we have not got any milk.'

'Well,' he said, 'we will soon have plenty!'

And from that day on till the two old aunties died John never left them again. That farm grew the most prosperous farm in the whole district. When the two old sisters died they left the farm to John Broom. And John Broom stayed there for the rest of his days; he had the biggest farm in the district. But no one ever knew where John Broom came from!

And that is the end of my story.

The Dog and the Peacock

The old collie dog was tired. He'd wandered around the village all day seeking little pieces of meat to eat from anyone who would help him. He'd wandered the village in fact for years. No one owned him, to the village folk he was just 'the old collie'. He was an old dog, disregarded, forgotten by his owner. But he was loved and respected in the village. Whenever anyone had a tidbit to spare it was always the old collie who would get something to eat. He slept here and slept there, he was a friend to the children, a friend to everybody. All the cats, dogs, everyone in the village knew him. He never touched no one.

But one particular evening the old collie got up from his sheltering place where he lay and it was cold. He thought to himself:

'I'll wander down the village and see if my old human friends'll give me something to eat.'

He wandered round the village and round the village two or three times, but lo and behold he never met a soul because everyone was indoors. The evening was getting darker and everyone had their Christmas trees up, their Christmas lamps going. And the old collie thought to himself:

'It must be Christmas. People are all in celebrating their Christmas Eve.' He said, 'I'll go down and have a talk to my old friend the peacock. Maybe he has something lying in his dish that'll help me.'

So he wandered down the street to a large bungalow owned by a merchant. And this merchant had two peacocks, a hen and a cock. The old dog went through the hedge, came round the back of the bungalow and there sitting on a post was the peacock. The old dog spoke.

He said, 'Hello, Peacock!'

'Oh,' he said, 'it's yourself old Collie.'

He said, 'It is.'

He said, 'You're on your wander tonight again.'

'Yes I am, I am on my wander tonight again. But there's not many people around.'

'No,' said the peacock, 'there's not many people around. My master and his wife and children are busy celebrating the Christmas Eve. And my old wife is sitting on an egg in there in the shed. She's sat there all summer on it and I don't think she's going to make much off it with the way I see it. And I'm just sitting here watching the moon and stars coming up.'

The collie says, 'It's a funny evening, all these people celebrating their Christmas and the coming of Our Blessed Saviour among us.'

'True,' says the peacock, 'true. But there must be some other people who are not as well off as some of them.'

'That's true,' says the collie, 'very true – in particular one good friend I have – my old friend the old widow-woman who lives in the last cottage at the end of the village. I passed by an hour ago and her light was out.'

'Sad,' says the peacock, 'sad – why some people have so much and other people have so little.'

'I feel sorry for her,' says the collie. 'She's good to me and she shares anything she has with me whenever I go around, though little she's got to spare. But, I wish there was something I could do for her. She probably won't have a fire, she'll probably have no light, she'll probably have no food and no one will probably give her a thought.'

'It's sad,' says the peacock, 'very sad.'

Says the collie, 'I wish there was something I could do.'

'Well,' says the peacock, 'between us we probably could think of something. I'm doing nothing here all night just sitting on this perch. And I mightn't go in and talk to my old wife, she's too busy sitting on that egg.'

The collie says, 'Look, are those peats you have there?'

'That's my master's peats,' says the peacock.

'Man,' he says, 'if the old widow had a couple of these, it would really give her a good fire for Christmas Eve.'

'Sure enough,' says the peacock.. 'And I don't think my master would miss any if a couple went a-missing.'

They were sitting talking, discussing the problem, when who should come down but the village tomcat. He too was owned by nobody; he was just a large black tom, a friendly tom who walked the village and was everyone's pet.

'Well, you two,' he said, 'you are busy chatting away again?'

'Yah,' says the collie, 'we're just here chatting away and discussing this evening.'

'Well, let me into the discussion,' says the cat. 'What's the problem?'

'Well, our main problem,' says the collie, 'is the old widow-woman at the end of the village.'

'A-ha-ha,' says the cat, 'her I know well! I just passed her house barely half an hour ago. It looks dark, there's no light and seemingly no fire on in it.'

'That's what we're discussing, that's our problem,' says the collie. 'The peacock and I have made up a plan here.

Peacock thinks that he could manage to get a couple of peats, take a couple up to the old widow-woman's house and give her a wee fire for Christmas Eve even though she has nothing else.'

'Well,' the cat says, 'she's good to me, she treats me very well; whenever she's got a wee drop milk or a bone to spare or anything she has for eating, she always shares it with me. And I would like to help.'

'But,' the peacock says, 'what good is a fire to her when she has nothing to eat?'

The collie says, 'Wait . . . all the shops are closed for the evening. But I know a way into the back of the butcher's, a secret passage where I go in and help myself to some bones. And I could help myself to much more than bones if I needed to, but I always just take the bones he leaves in a bucket. That's enough for me. But there's sausages and meat of all description! And I'm sure the butcher wouldn't miss a string of sausages.'

'Fair enough,' says the peacock, 'you do that!'

'But wait a minute,' says the cat, 'how about me? You know I too have my secrets, though I'm a cat! I know a secret way into the back of the fish shop. And the fish man always leaves heads and tails in a bucket and I go in and help myself. But there are many more things than that – there's fish and kippers and herring and everything in the fish shop. If the old widow-woman could have a pair of kippers it would make a lovely supper for her tonight. And,' he says, 'I'll go for a pair of kippers!'

'And I'll go,' says the old collie, 'for a string of sausages, a large string of sausages.'

'I'll be waiting here at the gate,' says the peacock, 'and I'll have a peat under each wing. And we'll all go, we'll visit the old widow and spend our Christmas with her!'

Sure enough, their plan was made. Away goes the old collie. He isn't long gone when back he comes with a big string of sausages in his mouth. And he's keeping them high so's they'll no touch the road. Within minutes back comes the tomcat. Oh, he is a great big black cat! And across his mouth he has a pair of large kippers, carrying them nice and tender in his mouth in case they'll touch the ground. And there stands the peacock, a peat under each wing:

'Are you ready, gentlemen?' he says. 'Let's go!'

And away go the peacock, the collie and the cat marching up the street. Everybody was inside behind their doors watching their Christmas trees and having their Christmas Eve lunches. Nobody paid attention to the peacock, the collie and the cat on their way up the street. They hadn't far to go to the end of the village.

Now the old widow's house sat by itself and round it was a large hedge and a gate going into her garden. Up came the peacock, the collie and the cat. The gate was open. But sitting on the gate was an owl, a large tawny owl. The old cat and the old collie knew the owl well because he was another old fellow who flew around the village.

He said, 'To-hoo, to-hoo!'

'Hello, Owl,' says the dog taking care that the sausages shouldn't drop out of his mouth. 'We are bound for the widow's house.'

And the owl says, 'The widow is very poorly tonight. She's very hungry and she hasn't thrown me any scraps for two days and she has no fire.'

'Well,' says the peacock, 'we are on our way to give her her Christmas. The collie has got some sausages and the cat has got some kippers and I've got two peats.'

'I'll come too—I'll come too,' says the owl, 'I'll come too!'

He hopped off the gate on his two feet behind them and he walked.

And they all marched – the peacock, the dog, the cat and the owl – all walked up the path. And they came to the door.

Scratch-scratch, scratch-scratch, went the dog with his foot on the door. No answer.

Scratch-scratch-scratch, again went the dog.

They heard footsteps. And lo and behold the door opened and this was the old widow-woman. The dog could see right into the room and the fire was burning very low – very little on her fire.

'Oh,' she said, 'it's yourself old Collie Dog. It's Christmas, and I'm sorry I've little to give you.'

But the dog never said a word. He just walked in – followed by the peacock, followed by the cat, followed by owl. And they all came up in front of the fire. The old widow-woman closed the door, she came in behind them and she looked and she saw; the dog left down the sausages, the cat left down the kippers and the peacock left down the two peats.

'O my children, my children!' she said. 'You've brought me my Christmas.' She took the two peats, gathered all the coals together and put the peats on the top of the fire. 'Sit there,' she said, 'children. And you've brought me sausages and you've brought me kippers. Oh how wonderful, we're going to have a Christmas feast!'

She picked up the sausages, picked up the kippers, went back into the kitchen. And the dog, the cat and the owl and the peacock sat before the fire.

The peats began to kindle up. The shadows began to leave the walls, the room began to come cosy with the brightness of the fire. When lo and behold the peacock said:

'It's a lonely old house this for a lonely old woman – without a Christmas tree!'

'Well,' says the old dog, 'we can't find a Christmas tree.'

The peacock says, 'We can't find a Christmas tree? Of course we can – we'll find the nicest Christmas tree of all for the widow-woman. I have a Christmas tree!'

'You,' says the collie, 'have a Christmas tree?'

He says, 'I have the nicest Christmas tree of all.' He says to the owl, 'You didn't bring a present, but your eyes are bright! You sit by the side of the fire, Owl!' And he says to the cat, 'You sit by the other side of the fire, Cat!'

And the cat sits at one side, the owl sits at the other. The peacock turns his back to the fire and spreads up his tail – it covers the whole fireplace. He hears the old woman humming away to herself in the kitchen.

And lo and behold the next thing she walks through with a plate of kippers and a plate of sausages, one in each hand. And when she comes through she sees the light from the cat's eyes, the light from the owl's eyes, the peacock's tail spread across the fire reflecting light.

'O my children,' she says, 'you've brought me a Christmas tree, the most beautiful Christmas tree of all!' And she cried and wiped her eyes with her apron, she was so happy. 'My children, you are the greatest little friends anyone could ever have. And now we're going to sit down, we're going to enjoy our Chirstmas Eve lunch.'

And the old widow sat down with the peacock and the dog and the cat and the owl. They ate up the kippers and they ate up the sausages. And the old woman sat and told them stories, talked to them till she got tired. Then she said:

'Children, it's time for me to go to bed. But till the day I die, I'll never forget how my wonderful little friends gave me such a wonderful Christmas Evening.'

So, the old woman opened the door and the dog went out and the cat went out, and they bade the old woman goodbye.

Down in the village everyone was happy enjoying their Christmas Eve. No one ever gave the old widow-woman a thought but the peacock, the dog, the cat and the owl. And they had the most wonderful Christmas of all.

And that's the end of my wee story.

How the Spruce Became Evergreen

It was around Christmastime when a little robin was hopping through the forest. And some boys who were out playing saw the little bird. Robins are very friendly – wherever you are in the forest they'll always come up to you. And one of the boys, who was a wee bit wild and vicious, said:

'There's a robin!'

He picked up a stone, threw it and hit the little robin, broke its wing. It went fluttering away among the grass. The boys walked on, never giving it a thought.

So the little robin crawled out from under the grass. He knew he wouldn't be able to fly anymore, for many months to come, because his wing was broken. And it being the cold winter time he thought to himself:

'I'll have to find shelter, a place where I can sit and rest and find some food, where nothing can touch me.'

He lived in the forest where there were many many trees of all description; ash trees, willow trees, there were beech trees, oak trees, fir trees and all kinds of trees. So the robin's first thought was:

'I must go to one of the trees, ask them to give me shelter, because I can't go to humans – they'll just break my other wing.'

He pulled his little broken wing, trailed it behind him and he hopped through the forest. The first thing he came to was a large beech tree and he said to it:

'Please, Mister Beech Tree, please help me!'

And the beech tree spoke to the robin, 'What do you want, little bird?'

He said, 'Some wicked boys have broken my wing; it's broken and I need shelter. I wonder, could you help me? Could you let me shelter in your branches for a while till my wing heals?'

'Be on with you, be on your way!' said the beech tree. 'I've no time for you little birds – you come here, you pick my nuts and eat my seeds. Be on your way, I've no time for you little birds!'

And the poor little bird hopped through the forest, he hopped further and it started to snow. He hopped on further dragging his broken wing through the forest and he came to a large oak tree. The oak had many branches and many hollows, crooks and turns in which the robin could have found shelter:

'Please, Mister Oak Tree, would you help me?' said the little robin.

'What do you want?' said the oak tree.

He said, 'Some evil boys have broken my wing and I need shelter. Would you please let me sleep in some of your branches till my wing heals?'

'Be on your way,' said the oak tree, 'be on your way! I have no time for you little pests – you pick my acorns and eat all my seeds, sit on my leaves and whistle all day long. You are just a nuisance – be on your way!'

So the poor little robin hopped further on through the forest among the snow till he came to a fir tree, a larch:

'Please, Mister Fir Tree,' he said, 'help me! Help me, please!'

'What do you want?' said the larch.

'I need shelter for the winter time,' said the little robin. 'Some boys have broken my wing and I can't fly. And I wonder if you could let me sit in your branches for a while till my wing rests and heals itself?'

'Be on your way!' said the fir tree. 'I've no time for you little birds. You sit and you chirp, you pick my needles off and hop among my branches disturbing my cones and eating my seeds. Be on your way!'

The poor little robin couldn't find shelter anywhere. So he hopped on further and he came to a large ash tree:

'Please, Mister Ash Tree, help me, please! I'm just a poor little robin with a broken wing and I need shelter.'

'Be on your way!' said the ash tree. 'You little chirping creatures – I have no time for you. I know what you do; you eat my seeds, you sit and chirp, sing all summer and when the winter comes you don't do anything for yourselves – but seek to find shelter with us. Be on your way!'

The poor little robin hopped on its way, hopping among the snow dragging its wing. It knew in its own mind no one was going to give it shelter. At last it came to a small fir tree, a little spruce.

And the spruce grows very tight in its branches, where it's warm. The robin hopped up to the little tree and said:

'Please, little Spruce, would you help me?'

And the spruce said, 'What's the trouble, little Bird?'

He said, 'Some evil boys threw stones at me and I think my wing is broken. I've asked all the trees in the forest for shelter and no one will give me any help.'

'Is that true?' said the spruce tree.

'Yes, it's true,' said the little bird. 'They ordered me on my way.'

'Come, come,' said the spruce tree, 'that's not the way to treat a little bird. Little birds should be treated more respectfully than that. I have many branches in my tree which are fine and warm, and many seeds have fallen down which will never reach the ground and will never grow. Hop up on my branches, little bird,' she said. 'Cuddle in my heart and you'll find warmth. I will whisper in the wind and sing you beautiful songs.'

And the spruce lowered one of her branches down. The little bird hopped up and he crawled away into the centre of the little tree. He was warm and comfortable and there were plenty of seeds lying around which had fallen from the top of the tree.

But he didn't know that a woodland fairy had stopped to rest on the same little spruce tree on her way back to the forest, when she heard the conversation between the tree and the little bird. And she said:

'Those wicked trees!' She heard the robin telling the story, how the trees had ordered it on and wouldn't help it. 'Those wicked trees'll have to suffer for what they did to this little bird. But not you, my little friend,' she said to the spruce tree, 'not you.'

Then she flies on her way to the middle of the forest and who does she meet but the North Wind. The North Wind was one of her greatest friends, so were the East Wind and the West Wind and the South Wind. She told the North Wind the same story I'm telling you.

And the North Wind said, 'Terrible, terrible, terrible! Terrible that these trees would do that to such a little bird. But,' he said, 'they will suffer, I will see to it. Oh, they'll suffer! They'll be cold in the winter when I blow through the forest. I'll blow every leaf and every twig off them, every rotten twig and leaf the next time I pass through the forest. And *they'll* need shelter. But the little spruce tree I will leave alone. And her branches will be green the whole year round and beautiful, and she'll be the pride of the forest. Everyone'll love her.'

And lo and behold, the next time the North Wind blew

through the forest he blew every single leaf off the ash tree, the oak tree, the beech tree and every needle off the larch – left them naked. But the little tree, the spruce he never touched. He passed on softly, held his breath when he passed her by. And for all year round after that the spruce tree was green and beautiful.

The little robin sat there all winter through. His wing healed and got better. He lived on the seeds that fell from the little tree. And in the summertime he flew away to find a mate, make a nest and have little birds. But always in the wintertime he flew back and perched on the top of the little tree; before he settled down for the winter he sat there, whistled and sang to his heart's content, because the little spruce loved to hear the robin singing his beautiful songs.

So that's why till this day when people celebrate Christmas in their house, they always love to have a little robin on their tree.

And that is the story of the Christmas tree and the robin.

Rorrie and the Stag

Many years ago when Rorrie the Eagle was born in his nest high up in the cliffs he was only a wee, wee white ball of fluff, just like a wee chicken. His mummy and daddy reared him up till he became a great golden eagle. And then they flew away and left him. Now his nest is on this cliff high up on the cliff face and he cannot fly. He is big enough, but he cannot fly.

And he wonders to himself, looks down and sees all the things away below him in the valley. And he sees this deer, a wee baby deer. He says to himself:

'I wish I could be down there and walk about on the valley floor where that wee deer is, and I could enjoy myself as much as what he is doing.'

This wee deer was hopping about and playing, playing and enjoying himself on the valley floor. But Rorrie the Eagle was left in the nest, a full grown eagle. He could not fly. He kept looking at the wee deer, looking and looking, edging farther out and farther out, and farther – till he got right to the edge of the nest – it was built with sticks and things and some of the sticks broke.

Down goes Rorrie! Out over the cliff face. And he's tumbling and tossing, tumbling and tossing. But on the way down he managed to spread his wings and he landed softly right on the valley floor. He's flapping and flapping around trying his best to fly.

When who comes stotting round the corner but this deer, the baby Stag. He was not much older than Rorrie the Eagle himself, about three or four months old. And Stag seeing the funny thing flapping on the ground, this young baby eagle, he came over.

And the Stag started – round about he went, bumping Rorrie with his head and dancing on Rorrie with his feet, you know! And the Stag carried on.

The poor eagle, wee Rorrie's trying to fly, and really trying! But he could not. He was only learning to fly. Anyway, Rorrie managed to crawl in behind these two rocks where the Deer could not get him. And he stayed there all night. He was awfully afraid, shivering with fright.

But the Deer finally got fed up. He wandered away, went and started feeding among the grass, away back to his mummy.

But days passed and Rorrie hopped about the ground, spread his wings trying his level best. And one day he hopped up on top of a big rock. He spread his wings, saw all the birds flying round in the air, crows and pigeons and things. He says to himself:

'If they can do it, I can do it!'

So he flaps his wings, and he took off! He started to fly. From that day on he never looked back. He used to climb high up in the sky and make nose dives down. He taught himself all the tricks of flying, and Rorrie was the greatest eagle on the cliff.

As he grew big so did the Deer. And the Deer grew and grew till he grew into a full-grown twelve pointed stag. It was near the end of the year.

And Rorrie the Eagle grew and grew till he was the finest and biggest golden eagle on the cliff. He used to climb high up into the mountains, scream and dive, and say he was the King!

One day he was out hunting, circling around hunting for rabbits or voles or rats or weasels, anything he could get, mountain hare, partridge, anything he could kill to eat. When the first thing he sees round this bend is this great big Stag Deer. He dived down! He knew right away who it was – the Stag who had given him the leathering when he was a wee young eagle.

Rorrie started to fight with him. He dived down on him, tore him with his talons. And the Deer was rearing up, trying to tear the eagle with his horns. They fought a wild battle! But no, none of them won. So the Eagle flew away back up to the top of the cliff. And from that day on the two of them were bitter enemies. They could not look at each other!

But in these days, as you know, all the animals could talk to each other. And word spread round the mountain about Rorrie the Eagle and the Stag Deer, how bitter enemies they were. There were foxes on the mountain, there were white hares, partridges, other deer. And everyone knew that Rorrie and the Deer were enemies.

So one day the Stag was grazing on the valley floor when down swoops Rorrie, lands on the rock. And he says to the Stag Deer:

'Look, now me and you have been enemeies for a long, long while. So I think the best thing we can do is get our heads together, both of us, and try and plan something to suit us both. I've been fighting you, and you've been fighting me. And I cannot hunt and keep my eye out for you, and you cannot graze and keep your eye out for me! This carry on cannot go on forever.'

'Well,' says the Stag, 'if you admit that I'm King of the Mountain, I'll leave you in peace.'

'No,' says Rorrie the Eagle,' you must admit that I am King of the Mountain. And then *I'll* leave *you* in peace!'

'No,' said the Stag, 'that will not do. You know I am King! I'm the greatest, the greatest deer in the herd. And I'm the leader. I always lead my hinds and the rest of my deer to safety when any gamekeepers or any people come about.'

'Well, I do the same,' says Rorrie. 'I do the same thing.'

'Well,' said the Stag, 'there's only one thing for it! We must fight, fight a duel.'

'Well,' said Rorrie, 'it's up to you. If you think you're about to fight a duel with me, you're welcome to try. But there's one thing we must do – we must fight it on the top of the cliff – right at the top we're going to fight a duel.'

'Well,' says the Stag, 'that will suit me just fine!'

So, word of this great duel spread right through the whole mountain that the Stag and the Eagle were going to fight a duel on the top of the mountain. The rabbits got to hear about it, the foxes got to hear about, pigeons and all the kinds of birds heard.

So, the two being kings in their own right, they called peace among all animals for one day to see this great duel on the mountain. And all the animals gathered round in a great big circle on the top of the cliff. There were foxes, white hares, there were badgers, and wee voles, weasels, rabbits – everybody came in a big circle – high up on the mountain top.

The wee animals started to speak to one another. Up spoke the Fox:

'Look, I've heard about this fight, this arguing going on. And that Stag does not bother me. I like the Stag. I'm a fox, and he does not bother me. But I would not trust Rorrie the Eagle. Rorrie would swoop down on me in a minute and carry me off to the cliffs, eat me up!'

'Aye, he would do the same to me,' said the Hare.

'And me!' says the Weasel.

'And me,' says the Partridge.

Everyone agreed that the Deer would not do them any harm. So everyone was on the Deer's side it seemed. But up spoke the Rabbit:

'It's a sin,' he said. 'You are all against the poor Rorrie. I know what they're going to do, fight a duel. But it's not the kind of duel you are thinking of . . .'

'Ah, what are you shouting about?' says the Fox. 'What's the matter with you? You be quiet! Wouldn't the Eagle sweep on you, down on you in a minute? Take you away if he got the chance?'

'Aye, he would,' says the Rabbit. 'But I keep out of his way, and he keeps to his way.'

Then up spoke the Hare, the White Hare from the mountain: 'Look, somebody go and tell the poor Stag what's happening. You know that Rorrie will play tricks on him.'

No, none of them would go. None would go and tell the Stag what Rorrie was going to do.

So up spoke the wee Vole, just like a wee rat: 'If you are afraid to go to the Stag,' he said, 'I'll go and tell him.'

Up goes the Vole, runs through the grass. And the Stag's standing. Vole scratches at Stag's leg. Stag looked down. Vole looks up at Mister Stag.

'What is it?' says Mister Stag.

'You'd better watch yourself, because Rorrie the Eagle is up to some trickery,' said Vole.

And the Deer looks down, he sees the wee Vole:

'Well,' he said, 'I'll be on the look out for his trickery.'

He said, 'They're all up there planning against you, the whole lot of them – they don't really like you. They'd rather have the Eagle win, even though he's their bitter enemy and would sweep down on them anytime. But you, you never did any of them any harm, just peacefully grazing! And I came to warn you.'

'Thank you very much,' said the Stag. 'But I'll look out for Rorrie's trickery.'

So to the circle come the Eagle and the Stag. Rorrie the Eagle spreads his wings in front of the Deer.

'Now,' he says to the Stag, 'it's your choice; what is it going to be?'

'Well,' says the Stag, 'I'm the fastest runner on this mountain. And you're the fastest flyer. Right, you see thon rock on the valley floor? I'll race you to the rock and back. And if I win, I'm the King! If you win, you'll be the King.'

'Okay,' says Rorrie. Rorrie was up to something false. So he says to the Fox:

'You come over here, Mister Fox, and you count three. When you count three, we'll set off!'

The Fox counted, 'One, two, three!'

And away they set. But the Eagle did not bother. He could have just glided straight across in minutes and land on the rock. But he did not want to do that. So he let the Deer win the race.

The Deer raced to the rock, turned and came back up. Rorrie just flapped his wings right along and flapped his way back. But the Deer ran down, turned at the rock and came back up to the top of the cliff before you could say 'Jack Robinson'.

'Now,' Rorrie says, 'you are the King of the Mountain! You won the race. But you cannot do what I can do!'

'I can do anything!' says the Stag.

'Well,' Rorrie said, 'if you are the King of the Mountain now, you must be able to do what I can do. If you can beat me then you are really King!'

'Right,' says the Deer, 'I'm willing.'

So Rorrie walked over to the cliff face. He skimmed right out over the cliff and landed slowly on the valley floor.

And the Deer said, 'If he can do it, I can do it!'

And he went straight out over the cliff face. He dropped right down to the valley floor and was killed. Killed on the valley floor.

And all the animals said, 'Well, that's the end of the duel.'

And they all went back to their own wee places. The Eagle remained the King of the Mountain. And that is true to this day.

This is an old Gaelic story, supposed to have been true.

The Four Winds

Away in the far north of Scotland a long time ago Jack lived with his old mother in a little rundown croft that he inherited from his father, who had been an alcoholic and drunk himself to death. He'd been a peat cutter, cut peats for a living. But because he had died when Jack was very young Jack had no clue how to cut peats.

Now, Jack's mother was not very old when his father died and she knew that she had to bring up her baby son alone. Oh, she told him all the wonderful things and told him all the wonderful stories. In her little house with the thatched roof made of heather life was very primitive. Anyhow, Jack and his mother had a good life together. But Jack had one problem.

Where Jack lived there was a moor, and that moor was covered in heather. Twice a year Jack would go and pull the heather to thatch his mother's house. Heather was very popular in these bygone times and many people thatched their houses with it. Those who could not afford to get heather, or it was too far to take it, used straw or bracken or something else. Jack was very lucky because his little house was near a heather moor. It wasn't much of a problem to Jack to pull the heather and thatch his mother's roof to keep out the storms and rain. But Jack's problem, his enemy, was the North Wind.

As you know, there are four winds, the East Wind, West Wind, South Wind and the North Wind. The rest of the winds were kind to Jack when they passed over his little house. But the North Wind seemed to take a dislike to Jack in some way. Every time he flew over Jack's house he blew the heather off the roof. Even though Jack tied it down, pegged it and thatched it and did his best, every time the North Wind passed he blew the thatch off. Now, when someone keeps doing these things on you it gets a little upsetting! So, every time the North Wind blew Jack got very upset.

One evening he sat by the fireside, the peat fire with his mother; he says, 'Mother, the North Wind must hate me. Because every time he passes over my roof he blows the heather off. I'm getting a little fed up.'

But she says, 'Jack laddie, listen to me. It's the North Wind and there's no much you can dae about it.'

'Oh aye, Mother, there's much I can do about it! I'm gaun down tomorrow to my old auntie.'

It wasn't really his auntie, but he called her this. She was an old hen woman. Now hen women were people who were very clever and they could foretell many things. They knew a lot. And Jack had carried down eggs from his mother and a wee bit o' cheese and things for the old hen woman because she lived all alone. She dabbled in herbs and cures and things like this, helping people. She was a wonderful old woman.

So Jack says, 'Mother, can you tell me something?'

'Aye, laddie, what is it you want to ken?'

He said, 'Mother, whaur in the world does the North Wind go when he passes ower my house? He must rest somewhere.'

'O laddie, that I cannae tell you. Ye ken there're four brothers – the North Wind, the East Wind, the South and the West Winds. But the North Wind is the most powerful one of all.'

'Well,' he says, 'it's him I want! I'm just sick fed up with him blowing the heather off my roof. If I could only get my hands on him, Mother, I would teach him a lesson he would never forget!'

'Ah well, laddie, is that possible? Naebody sees the North Wind. Only a pig can see the wind.'

'Maybe my old auntie would help me. Give me half a dozen eggs!'

So his mother gave him half a dozen eggs and a wee bottle of milk. And he put it in a wee basket and walked away down the moor to a little white thatched cottage. It was thatched with heather forbyes, but was neat and tidy. The wind had never touched it! And when he got down there, there lived old Maggie.

People called her Maggie of the Moss, because the moss is a moor. She collected all these herbs and made these moss wreathes and ferns for people who wanted to buy them. People thought she was a witch. People thought she worked in magic. But Jack knew better. She was just a friendly, good, old lady. And Jack loved her very much. So, he always used to visit her now and again. But this time he visited he had something on his mind. He wanted to know about the four winds. So when he got to the little thatched house old Maggie welcomed him.

'O Jack my laddie,' she said, 'it's yourself! Come on in. It's two-three weeks since I've seen ye.'

And she brought him into the house and gave him a wee cup of tea which she boiled in her kettle on the peat fire. Jack sat by the fireside.

She said, 'Jack, I'm glad to see ye.'

'Well, auntie, I'm glad to see you too. You see, I have a problem.'

'Well, what's your problem, laddie?'

'Auntie, it's the North Wind.'

'O laddie, the North Wind! Now what has he been doing to you?'

'Auntie, look, I try my hardest. Every time the East Wind, the South Wind and the West Wind blow over the house they never dae any trouble. But when the North Wind comes he keeps blowing the heather off my roof. It disna matter how much I try, he keeps blowing the heather off! I'm sick fed up thatching the roof just for him to blow it off again. Auntie, I want you to help me. I want to catch the North Wind!'

'O laddie, laddie, you're asking for something ... something! Ye ken there're four of them, and they're powerful brothers. And Jack, look, you'll only get yirsel in trouble.'

'Never mind, auntie,' he says, 'just tell me! I want tae find the North Wind.'

'Oh well, laddie,' she says, 'if that's what you want. I'm here to help ye. I'm your auntie and I like to help ye. Look, high above your house is a cliff two miles from where you stay, Jack. And high on the top of the mountain is a cave, a stane cave. Wonst a night the North Wind comes to rest there before he travels on his journey north after he passes ower you.'

'Good enough!' says Jack.

And she says, 'He only rests there for a few minutes. Look, it's you and him for it! But I'll tell you, Jack, you'd better watch yourself. Because you ken the North Wind is very powerful!'

'Aha,' says Jack,' dinnae worry! That's fine, auntie.'

So he sat and cracked with her for a wee while longer, had another bit cake and a bit tea and bade his auntie good night. Off he went home. His old mother was still up and out of bed when he got home.

'Well,' he said, 'Mother, I learned what I wanted to learn.'

She said, 'What did you learn now, laddie? Did your Auntie Maggie help you?'

'Aye, Mother, she helped me. She tellt me whaur I can catch the North Wind.'

'Oho laddie, laddie, I thought she would! But ye ken you'll have problems.'

'Oh well, Mother, I've made up my mind. And it's the North Wind I can catch because me and him's got a bit of an argument. I know what I'm tae dae.'

So next morning after breakfast it was a calm, calm day. There was not a breath of wind in the whole air. But that didn't deter Jack in any way. He went into the barn. They had a little barn beside his little croft where they lived. He got a piece of stout rope. And he got a sandwich from his mother and a wee bottle of milk. He bade his mother good-bye.

'Mother, I don't know for how long I'm going.'

She says, 'Laddie, where are you going?'

He said, 'I'm gaun to catch the North Wind!'

And the old woman shook her head. 'You'll come back a sorry, sorry, mair sensible laddie.'

'Well, Mother, it'll no matter. But I'm still gaun.' And Jack set off.

He made his way and climbed that mountain. Up and up he went for mile after mile until he came to a clift face, a steep clift face, and Jack looked up.

Sure enough, on the face he could see an opening of a wee kind of cave affair. But with the help of the rope Jack managed to loop it over the rocks and climb up. He got into the little cave. Bare stone floor, no bigger than this little room was this stone cave.

'Ah,' says Jack, 'old Maggie was telling the truth!'

So he went into the corner and there he sat and waited. He

waited and he waited. Then he heard a souch comin across the land, a kind of a breeze. And Jack's sitting there in the corner with the rope in his hand when he heard a plop in the front of the cave.

In walked a wee fat man with a round, red cherry face and puffed out cheeks! And Jack grabbed him. He wrapped the rope around him.

'Aha,' he says, 'I've got you!'

The wee man looked at him. And his round fat, cherry red cheeks:

He says, 'What's wrong with you, young man? What is it you're after?'

Jack says, 'I've got ye! You have been passing ower my house and blowin the heather off my roof. What's the reason? What have I done to you? You're the North Wind!'

'Ah no, no, laddie,' he said. 'You've made a big mistake. It's no me you're after. I'm the East Wind!'

Jack said, 'You're lyin' to me!'

'No,' he said, 'I'm no lying to you, laddie. I have nae reason to lie up to you. I know why you're here. But I'm the East Wind. I never hurt nobody. I blow softly over land and blow the pollen from the flowers, blow the blossoms from the trees. I'm the East Wind.'

Jack said, 'I believe you,' because he was so pleasant, the old man. 'Well, look, I'm here to catch the North Wind!'

'Aha, I ken who you're after,' said the East Wind. 'You're after my big brother. But, Jack, you might have a bit of a problem.'

So the East Wind sat with Jack. Jack took the rope off him, loosened it off. He cracked to Jack, tellt him all the wonderful stories of the places he had been, travel all over the country and all the beautiful things. Jack began to like the East Wind. After a short crack the East Wind said:

'Well, Jack,' because Jack tellt him his name, 'I have to be on my way.'

And Jack bade the East Wind goodbye. Then he was gone!

Jack sat there a wee while. Then he heard a calm souch comin, come across the clift once more. Then there was a humming sound and in walks another wee fat man! But he was dark of eyebrow and black of eye and small of face. He landed on the floor. Jack flung the rope around him! And tied him up.

'Young man,' he said, 'what are you doing?'

He said, 'You've been blowin over my house takin the heather off. And every time I thatch my roof you blow the heather off! What's the reason? What have I done to you?'

The wee man said, 'I think, young man, you've made a big mistake! I never blew your heather off your roof.'

Jack said, 'You're the North Wind, aren't you?'

'No, young man,' he says, 'I'm not the North Wind. I'm the West Wind. I know who you want. It's my big brother, the North Wind.'

So Jack sat there and they talked. He talked to the West Wind. And the West Wind told him how he travelled and blew the ships to sea and the wonderful things he had done. Jack was very happy with the West Wind.

'Well, young laddie,' he said, 'it's not my problem. It's your problem. I'll tell you, you'll have to be very careful. Because the North Wind is wir big brother. And you'll have a lot of problems.' So at last he said goodbye to Jack and off he flew once again.

Jack sat, made up his mind he would not leave the cave. Now he had the secrets of the two winds he had met, the East Wind and the West Wind. Then he sat. Here was a calm souch comin in.

And in came the South Wind! He was an old man with

grey hair hanging down his back, a long grey beard and a long narrow face. Gently he came down and he landed on the floor. The moment he landed Jack wrapped the rope around him! Once again. Pulled him in!

'What's this, what's this?' says the old man.

Jack said, 'I've got you!'

'Young man, what's your problem?'

'I've got you! You've been blowing the heather off my roof.'

'Jack, you've made a big mistake, young man. It's not me you're looking for,' said the old man.

Jack said, 'You're the North Wind!'

'No, young man, I'm not the North Wind. I am the old South Wind. And I have never harmed you in any way.'

And Jack took the rope off him. Jack sat there with the South Wind. The South Wind told him all the wonderful stories and the wonderful places he had been, and the things he had seen. Jack began to like the old man very much.

'But alas,' says the old man, 'young man, I have to go on my way! But be very careful. Because maybe tonight you'll have a visitor!'

Jack said, 'The sooner the better!'

And then the South Wind was gone.

Jack felt very lonely when the three winds had passed. Now he had met the three brothers. There's one more brother to come, the most powerful of all:

'The one,' said Jack, 'who's blown the heather off my roof. And he's in trouble. Trouble.'

Now Jack was a powerful young man himself. But there was a flash of lightning in the sky. A rattle of thunder! And a flash of lightning again. Then the storm began to blow. And the gale blew past the cave where Jack was, and the whistle of the cold North Wind.

'Aha,' says Jack, 'he's on his way!' He huddled in the corner.

Then there were footsteps came in: into the cave walked the fattest and most powerful little man Jack had ever seen, with a hard, red rosy face and long hair down his back! His eyes were staring as he walked into the cave. And the moment Jack saw his back he wrapped the rope around him, legs and arms, and tied him securely.

He puffed and he blew and he blew and he blew, blew the leaves from the cave! Bits of stones fell from the wall. But Jack held on. He turned and he twisted, he whirled. But Jack held on! He tried his best to get loose. He did everything within his power, and that cave was like a torrent. But Jack held on! At last he subsided gradually. And he drew his breath.

He said, 'Well, young man, what is it you're doing to me?'

Jack said, 'I've got you! I've got you at last. I've been waiting here a hungry, long two days for you!'

Because Jack had eaten up his sandwiches his mother had given him and drunk his little milk. He was hungry. So the little man was tied securely hand and foot.

And Jack said, 'Look, the reason I'm here . . . I have met your three brothers.'

'Well,' said the North Wind, 'what's your problem?'

Jack said, 'I have never hurt you in all my life.'

'Get to the bottom of your point!' says the North Wind. 'What have you got me tied here for? I'm due up North! 'I've ships to blow and trees to tumble and steeples to blow down.'

Jack said, 'Not tonight! You'll be blowing nothing tonight! Because probably I'll never set you free again.'

'What have I done to you?' said the North Wind.

Jack said, 'What have you done to me? You've blown the

heather off my roof, my mother's roof. Every time you pass by you blow the heather off and I've got to go and collect more, keep thatching my roof time after time after time! And you ask me what you've done! What have *I* done to *you*?'

'Oh I see,' said the North Wind, 'you're the young man who owns the little croft in the valley.'

Jack says, 'That's right. And I live there with my mother. We've done no harm to you in a million years.'

'Well, young man,' he says, 'what is your name?'

'My name is Jack.'

'Well, Jack,' he said, 'come sit beside me and I'll tell ye a story.'

And this is the story that the North Wind told to Jack: 'Ye see, Jack, a long time ago there were four of us and we're still around today – the East Wind, the South Wind, the West Wind and me. We were happy living with wir mother. But we had an enemy. And our enemy, who hated me most of all was my grandmother. Ye see, my grandmother was the most evil woman in this world! And she made me like this. Now, I could hae been like my brothers, a nice gentle person. It was things that my grandmother did to me that made me like this – oh, I fly across the country and I blow when I get angry. I cannot help for getting angry! But you see I'm not angry because of the people, of the trees in the forest or the woods or the ships in the sea; I am searching for my grandmother! You see, I will never rest in peace or be calm again till she is banished from this world. And I must find her! I believe she's in your roof. And she can take many forms. The latest form she's taken, Jack, is an *Owl*. And she's in your roof! That's why I blow over, why I blow the heather from your roof. Because she's tooken sanctuary there. So the only way you'll give me peace of mind, Jack, *if you destroy that Owl*. Get her out of your roof! Then I'll leave you in peace.'

Jack said, 'That's a wonderful story.'

So he took the rope off. He set the North Wind free.

'Very well,' says Jack, 'I'll go back to my house, to my little home on one condition: if you will come *calmly* when the thatch is on my roof! And I will strip my roof bare – if there's an owl in my roof you can have it.'

'Wonderful,' said the North Wind, 'wonderful! It'll save me breath. It'll save me a lot of breath!'

So that night Jack went home and he spent the night with his mother. He could not rest. The next day he was going to strip his roof. So, after breakfast Jack climbed up on the roof and he took piece of heather by piece of heather by piece of heather . . . and then he saw the storm clouds gathering in the sky. He knew the North Wind was on his way!

Then the wind starts to blow. And Jack was casting the pieces of heather. They were carrying with the wind and he was casting the pieces. Till at last, he came to the last one set on the roof. Sitting there in the corner of the roof was an Owl! When Jack took the last piece of heather from the roof the Owl got up! And flew into the sky. Then along came the North Wind! And the North Wind blew and blew and blew the Owl. But the Owl vanished into the forest and was gone! But the North Wind blew on. The Owl and the North Wind were gone.

Jack was never to come into contact with the North Wind again. Neither did he come in contact with the *owl*. But he thatched his roof with heather and every time the North Wind blew over Jack's roof it was a calm souch.

As for the Owl – till this day, if you will look over and watch an owl in flight you will see that an owl can never fly straight. An owl always flies in a slant. Because till this day the North wind has never caught up with his old grandmother! And that's why the North Wind is still so powerful.

And that is the end of my story.

This story was told me by John Macdonald, the most wonderful storyteller of the travelling people. He was crippled from the 1914 war and went on staves. People would give him his bed and breakfast in return for taking care of their children when they went out to work. John could not read or write and had never been in school. And he had the most fantastic stories! Some of them went on for three nights. But he would say:

'Laddie, I cannae tell you the rest of yir story tonight because I've nae tobacco.' We would have to get a bit more tobacco. But if you had an old pocket knife or an old belt or something to give him . . . 'Okay, laddie, sit down there and I'll tell you the rest of yir story.'

If you gave him a wee present he would go on all night!

Seal Man

The man who tellt me this silkie story was old Duncan Bell.
He was a cobblemaster, made stone bricks out of granite.
He was also captain of my shinty team. His son and eight
daughters stayed in Furnace, where I was born and grew
up. We were the dearest of friends; he liked me because I
was called Duncan like himself. I fished with him, rowed
his boat and dug his worms. Then he'd tell me stories about
the seals. He got this one from his granny, said his granny
tellt him it. There were a lot of good storytellers among the
women, especially among the crofting folk.

On a small island on the West Coast a long, long time ago
Jack lived with his mother. He had a good going croft,
everything he needed in this world. Jack's father had died
and left him well off. And his mother kept a few hens and
ducks. That's all she did, take care of Jack all her life. Also
along the shore on this little island where they lived were a
lot of white houses, wee farm cottages. And mostly every
person along the shore kept a boat because fishing was a big
concern. When any fish were caught, they shared with each
other what they could not sell.

   Now his mother had an old friend, an old man called
Duncan MacTavish. He would come visiting, sit cracking
and smoking his pipe talking about old times. And Jack

liked the old man very much. But Duncan was a fisherman. He'd fished all his life. He had known Jack since he was a baby.

But the one love of Jack's life was the seals. Whenever Jack had the time to spare he'd walk along the beach collecting firewood, flinging out driftwood, collecting stuff. He was a kind of a beachcomber. But when the time came in the spring he would make himself a whistle from an ash tree. And Jack's enjoyment was sitting on the rocks playing his whistle to the seals. They would come round, gather round him. They would pop their heads up and sit up to the waves. Jack would play the whistle and Jack loved the seals to his heart. And he was always telling his mother about them.

His mother would say: 'There are many stories about seals, you see, Jack. They tell stories . . . that there's such a thing as *seal men*.

'Aye, Mother,' he said, 'I don't believe in seal men. If there are seal men I've never seen any.'

'Laddie, look, there's seal men! I remember my granny a long time ago telling me when she was a lassie she'd seen a seal man walking along the beach, and he disappeared in the water.'

'Ach, Mother, that's only granny's cracks, old folk's tales!'

'Well,' she says, 'laddie, it may be old folk's tales, but it's true; there's such a thing as *seal folk*.'

But Jack would not believe it, he'd never seen any. But anyway, he still loved the seals.

And old Duncan MacTavish used to come along maybe twice a week. As Jack loved the seals old MacTavish hated them. He hated seals more than anything in the world! The only thing he never did was shoot them, because he was not allowed to keep a gun. If he'd had a gun he'd have shot every one. Because old MacTavish used to set a net and do a lot of fishing. When the seals came into his net, tore it, he went raving mad. But if he got some fish he would bring along a couple to Jack's mother for her and Jack's tea.

One morning Jack was not too busy and the sun was shining. It was a beautiful morning. He took a walk along the beach to collect more firewood or pick up his dry stuff he'd flung out the day before. And he came round, back beside a rock, no far from old MacTavish's house in the direction to the left of his own little cottage. There to his amazement lying at the back of a rock with his head up on the shore was a young man! And he was dressed in this kind of droll, kind of dark furry looking clothes. Bare feet. And dark, dark curly hair. He was face down in some seaweed. And Jack stepped forward.

When Jack turned him over half of the side of his face was all damaged. The blood – you could barely see his face! And Jack got an awful fright. He thought maybe the young man had fallen off a boat or something. He listened to the man's heart – he could hear it thumping strong.

Jack said, 'He's still living!'

And being a young, strong man, Jack got the young man on his arm, put him over his shoulder. He hadn't far to go. He carried him up to his mother's house. Into his own room, and he put the young man on the top of his bed.

'Oh!' and his mother cried, 'What happened? What happened, laddie, what happened?'

'Mother, it must have been an accident on the sea some place. Look, he's a young man. He's maybe been hit by a propeller of a boat or something. His head's in an awful mess.'

She says, 'Jack, wait a minute.'

The old woman ran in and got the big metal kettle on the fire. And she got water in a wee enamel basin. With a bit of cloth she washed the side of his head. And he was lying there. His face was pale. Dark curly hair.

She said, 'Jack, isn't he a handsome young man?'

'Aye,' said Jack, 'he is. But Mother, look, did you ever see the like of that?'

'What, laddie?'

'Mother, look at his fingers.'

And the old woman looked at the large snow-white hand. And his fingers were webbed like a duck's feet. In between his fingers were webbed. And Jack looked at his toes. It was the same thing. They were webbed too.

'Jack, brother dear,' she said, 'that's a *seal man.*'

'Nah, Mother, that's no a seal man. I heard my father tell me that you get folk born like that – with the skin between their fingers.'

'No, Jack,' she said, 'that's a *seal man*, laddie. God bless us, don't tell anybody!'

So the old woman went and she bathed his face with water and she had some kind of old spirits in the house. Then she patched it with goose grease and put a bandage round his head, and she left him comfortable lying on the top of the bed.

'Come on then, Jack, let him rest a while. And I'll make you a cup of tea.'

But lo and behold they hadn't sat down long to make a cup of tea when along came again old Duncan MacTavish. He had two-three fish on a string. And as usual he was in a raging mood. He came in.

The old woman said, 'Are you going to have a cup of tea, Duncan? We were just going to have a cup.'

'Tea?' he said, 'I'm not thinking about tea! If you could only see the mess of my nets, Mary. Have you seen the mess? You've no idea! With these blinking seals. God, that I was rid of them. They tore my nets. It will cost me a fortune to get them fixed. If I had a gun I'd shoot them all. But I'll tell you one thing, there's one of them will never bother me again. One of them will never trouble me!'

And the old woman said, 'What way? What happened?'

'Well, I'll tell you what happened; I got one of them today tangled in my net. And I got a right crack at him with a bell hook! He went down into the deep. And that was the end of him anyway. That's one of them anyway!'

But Jack and his mother never said a word. But Duncan gave them the two-three fish. And he walked away.

'Mother,' he said, 'do you think . . . are you thinking what I'm thinking?'

She says, 'Jack, didn't I tell you – that's a *seal man*. And you'd better not tell anybody.'

'O Mother, I'll tell nobody, not for the world.'

And she says, 'For God's sake, not a word to old MacTavish about this!' So the mother and Jack sat and had their tea. They cracked a long long while.

She says, 'Jack, do you think . . . we'll go and see that young man and see what like he is.'

They went up to the room. The bed was empty. He was gone! Jack searched the house far and wide.

'But, Mother, where could he go to? We could have hid him.'

She said, 'He must have slipped away while we were talking to old MacTavish.'

And Jack ran down to the beach. Nah, he wasn't there. He ran along the shoreside, round the house, searched the sheds. Nah, he was gone! The young man was gone.

'Well,' Jack said, 'at least we know he's not dead anyway.'

But two days later, after the young man had gone away, along came a commotion of a dozen folk from the village.

They were searching the shores. Jack ran down and asked what was the trouble. They said that they had found old Duncan MacTavish's boat. It had come in floating from the tide upside down. He was lost at sea. They found old Duncan's boat and they searched it. Then they searched the sea with boats for days and weeks. But old MacTavish's body never was found. He went a-missing.

Now Jack stayed with his mother for many many days, many many weeks. And the conversation was always about this young man. But Jack still continued playing his whistle to the seals. It never changed his life any, what had happened. But he always had one thought in his mind, if only he could have talked to him and spoke to him, asked him where he came from. Jack would have loved to know.

But anyhow, the weeks passed into months and the months passed into a year. And it was summertime once again. This was the time that Jack liked best. Because he could walk to where the sappy soukers grow along the shoreside. And he sat down one day with his knife and made another whistle with the bark off the sappy ash branch. After he got the whistle dried and cleaned, took all the sap off and put the bark back on he would begin to play a wee tune. And he would go down to the rocks and sit there, play his whistle on the rocks. But he always had the thought in his memory: I wonder what happened to the wee seal man that I carried up from the beach.

When he looked – up came half a dozen seals right out in front of him, not very far away! And this one came up a bit closer. They came in close to Jack not more than about five or six feet away. They stood there and watched him.

And one came up to Jack's waist and put his head from side to side. Jack could see a grey white patch round the side of its head. The hair had turned white, snow white on the side of his head. And it watched Jack for a long long while.

Then Jack stopped the whistle – and like that – the seals were gone. Jack felt awful sad at heart.

He said to himself, 'I'll never see him again. I'll never even speak to him! But at least I know he's still living.'

And he went back and tellt his mother the story I'm telling you: he said, 'Mother, you wouldn't believe what happened!'

'What? You never saw him again?'

'Aye, Mother! I saw him again.'

She says, 'Do you believe me now, Jack – he was a *seal man*?'

'Aye, Mother,' he said, 'it was a seal man.'

And Jack lived with his old mother there till his old mother died. He lived in that croft all his life, but he never again had a chance to see the seal man.

And that's a true story.

Fiddler's Doom

Many years ago, long before your day and mine there lived an old farmer and his wife on this sheep farm away in the West Coast in Argyllshire. They had a daughter, the most beautiful young girl. The sun rose and set on her; there was nothing in the world this girl could really do wrong! If she needed anything the father would say: 'I'll go to the market and get anything she wants.' If she wanted to help her mother in the kitchen the mother said: 'Don't do that, darling, let Mummy do it for you!' She was so appreciated, she was just *it*. The girl loved all this affection from her father and mother, but there was one affection they couldn't give her – love from somebody else.

Now Jack stayed in this wee croft across from the farm and lived with his old mother in a house. Many's the day Jack used to go whistling, pass by and see this bonnie lassie sitting by the fence. She never spoke. And Jack had this notion some day he was going to crack to her.

But even with all the affection from her father and mother the lassie began to get a bit lonely. So one day she came walking down and saw Jack sitting on the gate at the brig. He was making a whistle out of a bit ash – when the tree is young you slip the bark off and make a whistle from the bark like Peter Pan's – a very old tradition. Jack was sitting whittling away as fast as he could. After he made the whistle he started playing it.

This lassie, a beautiful girl about eighteen years of age, stopped. And Jack still played on. She listened to Jack playing the whistle. When he was finished she said:

'That was very nice.'

'Did you like that tune?' These were the first words he ever said to her. 'I can play many, many more tunes.'

'Well,' she says, 'play me some more tunes.'

So Jack played the whistle to her. And he played, he played and he played. The more he played the more the lassie fancied him. So Jack and she got to be good friends. Every day she slipped away to meet him at the gate at the brig and he played the whistle to her. But he played the whistle to her more ways than one . . . he played the whistle to her once too often!

But anyway, his mother said: 'Jack, I see a change coming over you, laddie. You're not the same person that you used to be.'

'No, Mother, I'm no the same person I used to be. Look,' he said, 'I think, Mother, I'm in love.'

'Oh, you're in love, are you? What way, who are you in love with?'

He said, 'Look, Mother, I'm in love with that lassie up in the farm.'

'O Jack, Jack, son, ye don't understand! Look, these people are rich, the richest farmers in the glen and they own the whole glen; they even own the land I'm living on! And you tell me you're in love with their daughter?'

'Mother, it's more than love.' He said, 'We've had a connection.'

'Oh, curse my soul, laddie,' she said, 'you're in trouble. Laddie, ye can't have anything to do with that lassie! That lassie on that farm up there is miles better than you.'

'But, Mother, you're too late now speaking about these things,' he said, 'we've had wir fun.'

'Lord upon my soul, laddie, you're in trouble!'

But anyway, time passed by. She never turned up at the gate. Jack sat, played his whistle and played his whistle, but she never came back. He played to his heart's content but she never turned up. Jack got fed up playing the whistle:

'Well, if I can't have her,' he says, 'I'm going to have nobody else.'

So next day he told his mother, 'Look, Mother, I'm fed up. I loved and loo'd that lassie, and she doesn't want to marry anybody. I really liked her. You're all right, you've got your house and my father left ye a wee bit o' money, ye can take care o' yirself. I'm going to leave, I'm going on my way, away tae seek my fortune in this world.'

'Aw, Jack brother,' she said, 'ye can't leave yir auld mother!'

'Aye, I'm going to leave my mother,' he said. 'Look, there's nothing for me here. The lassie doesn't want me anymore or she'd hae come back tae me.'

'Jack,' she said, 'you're lucky to be free o' these things – ye dinnae ken what trouble ye've done. Did ye have nothing tae dae wi the lassie?'

'Of course I had something tae dae wi the lassie!'

'Well upon my soul,' she said, 'you'll no hear the end o' it!'

Jack said, 'Mother, I'll come back in my own time.'

So the next day Jack packs his wee bundle on his back and away he goes. He left and cleared out.

Now the lassie sat with her mother, and her father said to her: 'Lassie, how ye walking away? You've been walking every night and carrying on, going away. I hope you've never been visiting any boyfriends or anything.'

'Oh no, Daddy,' she says, 'I'm not!'

But she began to get bigger and bigger. It got she couldn't hide it any longer – she was pregnant. The father and mother felt ashamed of this because their daughter wasn't married. And her daddy used to go to the market every day and discuss with all the farmers, because he was the landowner. The young farmers used to come courting but she wouldn't even look at them. She stayed in her room all the time, wouldn't even come down to the kitchen when anyone came visiting.

'Where's this lassie o' yours?' a young farmer would say.

'Oh, she's up in her bedroom, she'll no come doon.'

Then, one day she had a baby, the bonniest wee boy in the world. But there was one thing wrong, it had a hump on its back, its shoulder was out on its back – a hunchback! And the grandfather and grandmother were so ashamed of this! They hid it out, wouldn't tell one single soul. But the mother took care of the baby . . . they never told one single soul about it.

Now the old grandfather was a great fiddler. There was nothing in the world he loved better than playing the fiddle. He always played before the baby was born; but after, he had no time to play because he was too much worried that somebody was going to find out his daughter had a wean and wasn't married. He hid his fiddle up in the roof, never told a single soul about the baby or the fiddle!

But days passed by and the wee boy grew up. The old man loved him like nobody in the world even though he had a hunched back, and the old woman loved him too. But they hid him out, wouldn't show him to anybody because they were ashamed. But the daughter, the mother of the wee hunchback, a beautiful young woman, all in her mind she was thinking about the young man she had met at the gate playing the whistle.

Many's the time she walked down to the gate after her baby was born . . . when the baby was nine months old, a year old . . . Jack was gone. She walked past the gate, sat at the gate and cried at the gate, but Jack was gone. Jack never had one single idea he was father of a wee baby!

So anyway, time passed by and he grew up from two to three, three to four and from four to five – five years passed by. Jack never came back, Jack was gone.

But one day the wee boy was up in the roof, in the attic raiking around looking for toys while his old grandfather was out cutting the hay. He comes across the fiddle and the bow belonging to his grandfather up in the garret! And he takes the fiddle, and he had a good idea – he puts it across his knees. He pulls it, hears this bonnie noise, pulls the bow across the strings and hears this bonnie noise. But he doesn't know how to play it. It was amusement to him. So that night when his grandfather comes back after cutting hay all day he takes the fiddle and the bow, goes down the stairs from the attic to the living room.

He says, 'Granddad, this is a thing that makes a bonnie noise.'

'Aye son, it really does, it really makes a bonnie noise. But,' he said, 'come here, laddie, and I'll show ye how to make a better noise!'

So the old man takes the fiddle, puts it under his chin and starts to play. And the wee laddie gets so interested.

'Granddad,' he said, 'that's beautiful, that is the best in the world!'

So he shows the wee hunchback how to play the fiddle! And this wee laddie learns to play the fiddle, plays well, plays it well because his granddad teaches him.

But as good as his granddad teaches him, it isn't good enough. He has that ambition to be better than his granddad. While his granddad is away cutting the hay every day the wee laddie takes his fiddle below his oxter, and his bow, he goes away out to the moor and practises playing the fiddle. Now he's about six.

So one day it was the very first day, the very first morning in May. He goes out with the fiddle below his oxter, walks away past the farm way over by the hill and he comes to his bonnie wee hillock, a wee knowe. He sits down upon the knowe. He thinks he's going to sit and practise his fiddle the way his grandfather told him, so he could play a bit to his grandfather. Sitting on the wee knowe he's playing away on the fiddle under his chin.

But he hasn't played for very long when all in a minute he's surrounded by all the *wee people*, all the wee folk in the world standing around him, about a hundred and fifty *wee people*. And he stops, lays the fiddle down, scratches his head – he's only a wee boy!

'Please, little people, please leave me alone. I was doing no harm,' he said. 'I'm only playing my fiddle.'

And the one who was chief of the *wee people* said, 'Look, son, we're not here tae harm ye in any way. We loved your music but you're not playing the fiddle very good.'

And the wee boy said, 'Aw, I'm only playing the way my grandfather taught me.'

'Well,' he said, 'your grandfather can teach ye a lot, but we could teach you better.'

And the wee boy said, 'Look, could you teach me better tae play the fiddle?'

'We'll teach ye better tae play the fiddle, but,' he said, 'ye'll have tae move, son, ye'll have to shift because we need this wee hillock! We need this wee hillock, ye see, for wirsels.'

The wee boy didn't want to be upsetting in any way, 'O little people, I don't want to insult yese, I don't want to bother yese in any way,' he said, 'I'll go, I'll go!'

'Oh no,' the biggest of the wee men said, 'ye don't need

to go away so quick! But we'll *give* ye something before ye go – and what is it you would really like?'

'I want nothing belonging to yese, little ones, I want nothing by you. I love youse little people!' he said, 'I have no friends tae play wi and I'm only living wi my grandmother and my grandfather. And I've never seen you little people before, I don't mean youse any harm.'

'I know ye mean us no harm. But,' he said, 'we're going to *give* you something.'

'Oh,' he said, 'I want nothing!'

'We're going to give you something that is going to last you for the rest of your life. And I hope,' he said, 'it will not be tae your sorrow!'

The wee boy said, 'Well, what are ye going to give me?'

'We're going to give ye a fiddle that is master. Go your way,' he said, 'and leave us in peace, and,' he said, '*you be the fiddle's master!*'

'Oh,' the wee boy said, 'well, I'll go!'

The wee boy said goodbye to the wee people, took his fiddle below his oxter and his wee bow in his hand and walked away. He walked home. By the time he got home his old grandfather was home. He milked the cow, brought in the milk and his old granny was making scones. He came into the kitchen. The wee toy laddie came in, sat down by the fire.

The old grandfather said, 'Play us a tune, play me a wee tune, laddie, like the way I taught you!'

The wee boy said, 'All right, Granddad, I'll play ye a tune.'

The wee boy put his fiddle under his chin and started to play. He played and played and the tears came rolling down from his grandfather's eyes. His old grandmother stopped baking and stood bewildered as if she was turned to stone! She had never heard anything in her life like the way the wee boy was playing. And the tears rolled down his grandfather's cheeks.

He said, 'Son, Grandson, where in the world did you ever learn to play like that?'

'Granddad,' he said, 'I'm only doing what you taught me to play.'

He said, 'I never taught you to play like that. But anyway, play me another tune!' And the tears – he wiped his eyes with a hankie – this wee boy started to play again.

But the post always came up from the village, and because he had a long way to go up the glen to deliver letters it was always evening before he got to old John's cottage. It was night-time by the time the post had come to deliver the letters. When he stopped he heard the fiddle.

Now the post was a fiddler himself. He listened. And he heard the greatest music in the world that he'd ever heard in his life.

'It can't be auld John playing the fiddle, he couldn't play like that,' he said. 'I'm a fiddler and he's a fiddler but auld John couldn't play like that! There must be another fiddler in the house forbyes him.' So the post knocked on the door.

And the old woman said, 'Hide yourself, laddie, hide yourself!'

She was making the wee boy hide himself when the post walked into the house – he saw the wee laddie with the fiddle. He said:

'John, were you playing the fiddle?'

'No,' John said, 'it wasn't me; it was my grandson.' And then the secret was out.

'But,' he said, 'John, I didn't know ye had a grandson.'

'Well now,' said the old man, 'now ye know. Look . . .' and he told him the same story I'm telling you. 'My daughter had a bairn and he was a hunchback and we were ashamed

o' him. But we're not ashamed o' him anymore; I think he's
the greatest fiddler in the world.'

The post said, 'He is the greatest fiddler – look, he took
the tears tae my eyes and I was only standing at this door!'
He says, 'Play me a tune!'

So the wee boy started to play and the post cried like a
baby! He played and he played till the tears were rolling
down the postman's face.

The postman said, 'Stop, I can't take any more. Please, I
can't take any more. John,' he said to the old farmer, 'look,
that is the greatest fiddler that ever walked this earth.'

Now the postman goes away and he's got this in his
thoughts in his mind, 'Where in the world did that boy ever
learn to play, tae make music like that?'

Now naturally, in the village where he stayed they always
had a harvest home every year when the harvest was ready.
And a fiddler used to always play for the dancing. So, all
the people gathered in the village hall. They had a special
fiddler who used to play every year, but when they asked
him to come he was ill. There was no fiddler to play at the
harvest home.

And the old postman said, 'I can't play the fiddle as good
as what the fiddler who is ill could do.'

Somebody said, 'We have to have a fiddler, we can't have
a harvest home without a fiddler.'

And the postman said, 'I can get ye a fiddler, somebody to
play the fiddle like it was never played before!'

And the people didn't believe this, 'You're kidding us,
you're telling us lies!'

And the postman said, 'I can get ye a fiddler, a fiddler like
ye never heard in yir life before, who will make ye cry!'

They all said, 'Okay, you get him, postman, and let us
listen!'

The postman made his way up to the farm. He knocked on the door and old John came down.

'John, look,' he said, 'we're having a great harvest home. You're invited and your old woman.'

Old John said, 'I can't make it, no the night; no, me and my old woman can't make it.'

'Well,' he said, 'can we borrow your grandson tae play the fiddle for us?'

'I'm ashamed o' my grandson,' the old farmer said. 'I know he can play the fiddle . . . he's a hunchback!'

'You might be ashamed o' him but we won't be ashamed o' his music,' the postman said. 'Look, let him come and play for us tonight at the harvest home.'

So, they went to the young boy and asked him would he come?

And the boy said, 'Okay, I will. I'll go, play the fiddle at the dance. I've never played before; it's only music tae me, I'll play music for them if they want. I'll play the music!'

So, he and the postman walked down the glen, not far to the village and by the time they landed there the harvest home was just getting started. People were singing.

The postman walked in and said, 'Ladies and gentlemen, I want you to be quiet for a few minutes. I have brought to you tonight the greatest fiddler that ever walked this earth. He is not very old, he is so young!'

And everybody said, 'Who, who is it?' Nobody knew where he came from, nobody knew.

He says, 'He's going to play for youse tonight, ladies and gentlemen, and take the place of the fiddler who is not here to present our great harvest home.'

The young laddie started to play. He begins to fiddle. Everybody starts to cry and to greet and they start to scream. And they run up to him, try to fling their arms around him.

But when he saw that he got terrified – he thought they were going to do him an injury. He ran out of the hall straight through the door and across the moor. He ran and ran but the people ran after him wanting to bring him back – they wanted more music they loved his music so much. But the poor wee soul thought they were after him and were going to do him an injury.

And he ran and ran and ran and came to a bog; he went down into the bog and disappeared. He, fiddle and all.

When he went down the people said: 'He's gone into the bog! We were to blame.' And they all walked back and said, 'We'll never see the fiddler or hear his kind o' music again.'

And the little people stood beside the bog and said, *'He's gone from them but he's not gone from us, because we have taken him and he'll be with us for the rest of wir time.'*

The fairies got him and took him away for the rest of his days.

I heard that story a long time ago. My oldest brother told me that story when I was only young.

Jack and his Mother's Wee Puckle Corn

Jack stayed with his mother in this wee croft in the forest. But his father died when he was awful young, and he was reared with his mother. His mother was awful fond of him. She did everything in the world for Jack, just treated him the best she could. He used to take his two-three eggs to the town and sell them for his mother. And whatever coppers she got for the eggs she would say, 'Well, keep that two-three shillings to yersel.' And Jack never really did very much work or anything. But he helped his old mother round the croft as much as he could. They kept a cow and they sellt a wee drop milk. She sellt two-three eggs and managed to keep her and Jack the best way she could. But that's all Jack ever did – lying out in the sun, wandering here and there and helping his mother whenever she wanted. Anyway, years passed and Jack grew up. He grew into a strong, sturdy young man. Oh, a good-looking young man he was too!

When one day his mother says to him, 'Laddie, it's coming near noo the harvest time, Jack. And ye ken it's about time you were gaun to cut that wee puckle corn, or the auld coo'll no hae a bite in the wintertime. And nae meat for it means nae meat for me and you!'

'I'll dae it the morn, Mother,' he said.

'Never mind daein it the morn,' she says. 'Can ye no go oot and dae it noo, laddie? Look, I'll tell ye what tae dae. The morn I'll rise early and I'll mak ye a good bowl of porridge. I'll get ye up afore the sun rises. And you go oot. For aa the time it'll take ye, God bless us, laddie! When ye cut that wee puckle corn, there's no much in it, ye'll have aa the time in the world tae yersel. Ye can do onything you like! Gang to the toon or awa wander, wherever you want to go.'

'Oh well, Mother, if ye mak me a good bowl of porridge the morn and wauken me early, I'll go and gather my old scythe up. I'll see what I can dae.'

'Well,' she says, 'mind and dae it!'

So the next morning the old woman got up in the house and true as her word she rose about four o'clock, before the sun got up. She's on with this great metal pot. She made a great big pot of porridge and the best of sweet milk. She gave him a good breakfast. He sat a good while, cracked to his mother.

'Noo, Jack,' she says, 'the best thing tae dae – if ye manage to cut it aa in the forenoon – let it lie a wee while and gae back and stook it up in the afternoon.'

'Ah well, Mother,' he says.

'Because it might come a bad time o' rain,' she says, 'and we'll no hae a wee bite for the auld coo during the winter. We'll hae to sell her. And the minute we sell the coo we'll no hae nae milk! I cannae afford to buy milk.'

'Okay, Mother, I'll do my best! I'll no come back till I'm finished.'

'Well, see and dae that! But mind, if ye feel hungry, mind and come back. Come back early if ye feel hungry!'

But it was a nice morning. After he'd got his breakfast, his bowl of porridge and good jug of tea to himself, 'Goodbye, Mother,' he said, 'I'll see you about dinner time.'

'Right, laddie, and be careful when you're sharpening that scythe in case you cut yourself.'

'Aye,' he says, 'right!'

She was awful fond of him, feart of anything happening to him.

But away he goes whistling with the scythe on his back to the field. He had a good bit to go. There wasn't much corn, about an acre in the field. Oh, and it was beautiful corn. But where Jack had ploughed this field for his wee puckle corn for his mother's cow in the wintertime, and to make a puckle meal for him and his mother – was a knowe – a wee bit that couldn't be easily ploughed. It was all full of bonnie clover and daisies in the middle of the field. Jack had ploughed round it and sowed it with corn for his old mother in the spring of the year. Oh, and the lovely, beautiful corn was the height of your thigh. But the bonnie wee knowe in the middle of the field was too high. And this was the first year Jack had ever tried to plough it. Before, he'd always kept it in grass for the old cow.

So just as the sun began to come up, back of six o'clock in the morning, Jack walked round the wee field. And he walked up to the wee knowe. He stuck the scythe in the ground beside him:

'Ach,' he said, 'I'll wait for a wee while till the dew comes off the corn. I'll wait for half an hour till the sun comes out right before I start to cut.' And he sat down. But, Lord, O bless us! In five minutes' time he was surrounded with all these wee folk! Jack looked round him.

He says, 'In the name of the God, whaur did all youse come fae?'

They were fairies. About a hundred and fifty of them – fairies, all gathered round him on the top of the knowe. Jack was sitting on top of the knowe. He never saw them as they came out from among the corn.

And this, the biggest one, he came up. He was the king, the Fairy king!

'Aye, good morning, Jack!' he said. 'Ye're early.'

Jack didn't know what to say: 'God bless us, whaur did youse wee folk come fae?'

'Ah, Jack,' he says, 'we're fairies.'

'Ah,' Jack says, 'fairies! There's nae such a thing as fairies!'

'Well, we're fairies,' he said, 'and I'm the king. I'm the ninth generation o' thes fairies, this generation I'm in the noo. And we've come to celebrate, Jack, on this knowe. I'm sorry, you'll have to move!'

'Ah,' but Jack said, 'wait a minute! I've my wee puckle corn to cut for my mother's coo. I cannae hae youse wee folk running about the field celebrating through my corn while I've to cut it. In case I cut youse with the scythe! If youse is fairies?'

He said, 'We are fairies! Can you no believe yir ain een?'

'Oh, I believe my een. I see yese! I heard my granny, God rest her soul in heaven, and my father afore me speaking about fairies. But I never had the guid grace to see ony.'

'Well, Jack,' he said, 'many's the time we seen you at the distance for aa you've never seen us. Well, you'll have to shift!'

'Ah,' Jack said, 'I cannae! I've got to get this wee puckle corn cut.'

He says, 'Jack you're no gaunna cut nae corn the day.'

'Ah but,' he says, 'I am! I'm gaunnae cut the corn the day!'

'But Jack, tell me this, what do ye dae wi your corn after ye cut it?'

'Well,' he says, 'my mother feeds some of the shaifs to the coo And we send the rest to the miller to get made into meal.'

And he said, 'What do you do with the meal?'

'Well,' he said, 'we mak porridge. My mother maks me porridge and she makes bannocks.'

'That's it!' said the King of the Fairies, '*bannocks*. That's hit! That's the thing my great-great-grandfather in fairyland many, many hundreds of years ago said – that he got a bannock fae some o the humans – and it was the greatest thing in the worl. Jack, you'll have to mak me a bannock!'

'Ah, wait a minute,' Jack said. 'Look, it's my mother maks bannocks, no me!'

'Ha! But your mother's bannock's nae use!' he said. 'We're gaunna celebrate here. And through the ninth generation of kings, I'm the King of the Fairies. All my other generation – to my grandfather and my granny right through – everyone spoke about the *bannock*, whatever thing it is. I want you to tell me what it is! And I want you to mak me ane! Or there'll be nae corn cut for you this year!'

Now Jack began to get annoyed with this wee man. All the wee fairies are sitting round about. They're no saying a word. Women and men and laddies. They're only six inches high.

Jack said, 'Look, I've to get my mother's wee puckle corn cut!'

And the Fairy king said, 'I've to get a bannock baked! We're gaunna celebrate on this knowe on to noon.'

'Ah,' said Jack, 'I doot no! Look, call in your wee folk frae among my corn till I get a start.'

Says the Fairy king, 'What are ye gaunna cut it wi?'

'I'm gaunna cut it with a scythe.'

'Are ye?' says the king. 'I doot no, Jack! You're no gaunna cut that with nae scythe.'

'Hoo no?'

'But go on,' he said, 'try it! Go on and lift your scythe, and see hoo you get on.'

Jack said, 'I'll lift the scythe all right. For aa the fairies in the country I'll lift my scythe! And if ony o' your wee folk gets cut, blame theirsel – it's no my fault.'

Away he goes to the scythe. And he tries. He pulls and he pulls and he pulls. But na! If ye gave Jack all the money in the world he couldn't move the scythe. It stuck solid into the ground.

The Fairy king walked up and he sat, crossed his legs on top of a big clover. He says:

'Jack, ye mightna! Ye're only wasting your time. Now look at your corn. You're big and strong aren't you? You're Jack, and your mother over there feeds you well! Go and try and pull ane of these corns oot, one corn strae, try and pull it oot!'

Jack tried. He got one corn straw. Now the likes of me and you catching a corn straw, you just pull it with your two fingers. Jack got his arm around the corn straw and he pulled. He pulled and he pulled and he pulled. But nah!

'Ye mightna!' says the Fairy king. 'Ye mightna pull that. Because that'll no come oot wi ye, no the day.'

Jack said, 'Look, I've got to get this wee puckle corn cut! It could be rainin the morn.'

'Aye,' the Fairy king said, 'it's gaun to be rain the morn. And I'll tell ye better than that – it's gaunna be rainin the next three days after the morn! That's the way wir here the day. Thunder pumps for the next three days!'

'Well,' says Jack, 'what do ye want me tae dae? In the name of creation, what do ye want me to dae?'

He said, 'I want you to mak me a bannock!'

But Jack said, 'I cannae! I'll gang to ask my mother.'

'No,' he said, 'I'm no wantin you to ask your mother. I want *you*!'

But Jack said, 'I need meal, and I need milk and I need a fire. And I need my mother's girdle.'

'You get the meal and milk, and the girdle. We'll get the fire!' says the Fairy king.

'Right,' says Jack, 'if that's gaunna be, it's on your head. I'll mak it – but I've never made it before.'

The Fairy king said, 'Look, you've watched your mother makkin bannocks often. And I've seen her masel many times through the window makkin bannocks for aa she never seen me. We've been around, ye ken, Jack, we ken what goes on! And you can mak a bannock if you try. If you hadna been here, or your mother had hae been here instead o you, *she* would hae had to make the bannock! But you're the ane that's here and you've to mak hus a bannock to celebrate this day. And we want it afore noon. Before twelve o'clock.'

Jack put his hand in his pocket and took out his watch and looked; it was five minutes to seven in the morning. The sun was shining bright. He's no long after his breakfast, you see!

The Fairy king said, 'Right, Jack! You go back to your mother's hoose and get the meal, the milk and the girdle. And we'll get the sticks and kinnle the fire till you come back.'

Jack said, 'Look, you get sticks? There's nane o' youse as big as a fir cone!'

'Never you mind what like we are, Jack. You just do what you're tellt if you want your corn cut this year. You dae what ye're tellt!'

'All right,' said Jack. 'Be it on your ain head. And I hope it'll poison youse when youse dae get it! But there's only one cure for it.'

Jack goes back to the house. His old mother's in the kitchen working away. Now what has she got in the corner of the kitchen but a big barrel and a scoop for lifting the meal, a brass scoop.

She never heard Jack coming in. But he's searching around

for a sheet bag, ye ken, a bag for holding the meal in. It was flour bags they kept in them days. Nae paper. And she heard him rumbling in the barrel. She comes through.

She says, 'Laddie, in the name of God, what are you daeing?'

He said, 'Mother, I'm getting some meal.'

'What?' she said, 'I'm after feedin ye afore ye left. It's no a half an hour ago since you got your porridge and milk and plenty tea and scones.'

'Mother, I'm no hungry.'

'Well, in the name of God, laddie,' she said, 'hoo'd you no cut the wee puckle corn?'

'Mother, hoo can you cut corn?'

'What do you mean, hoo can you cut corn? You've a scythe to cut it, haven't you?' she asked.

He said, 'The wee folk running through my feet!'

'Aye, Jack, whatna wee folk? Laddie, you're *away wi the fairies*!'

'Aye, Mother,' he said, 'ye never said a truer word in your life. I am awa wi the fairies. That's true. I want meal. And I want milk. And I want your girdle.'

'What?' says his mother. 'Jack, are ye gettin moich? Ye're gettin kind o' droll.'

'I'm no gettin droll. Mother, I'm gaunna bake a bannock.'

'What?' she says, 'bake a bannock? You bake a bannock? Laddie, what's comin adae wi ye? Ye gaun aff the heid or something?'

'No, I'm no gaun aff the heid. I want to bake a bannock to the Fairy king.'

'Noo, you're really awa with the fairies!'

'Mother,' he said, 'look, if I dinna get a bannock bakit to the Fairy king there'll be no corn cut! And it's gaunna rain for three days.'

'Ah Jack, Jack, what's come ower you? Laddie, laddie!' said the old woman. Now she began to get worried. 'Laddie, laddie, what's come ower you? Hoo are you gaunna ken it'll rain for three days?'

'The Fairy king tellt me it's gaunna rain for the next three days.'

The old woman was in an awful state. She didn't know what to do.

'All right,' she says, 'Jack.' She was nearly in tears. 'Tak meal, tak milk and tak the girdle wi ye and bake the king's bannock. But for God's sake try and come to yersel and cut the wee puckle corn!'

'Mother, look, dinnae worry about me. There's naething wrong with me.'

She said, 'There's naething wrong with a full grown man runnin aboot a field o' corn wi a girdle to bake a bannock tae a fairy king? And ye tell me there's naething wrong wi ye!'

'Mother, it's aa right.'

'Oh, it's aa right!' she said. 'I ken there's something wrang with you. You never carried on like this afore in your life. *Fairies* – a full-grown man like you believing in fairies!'

'Never mind,' says Jack, 'Mother, you carry on with your work. And I'll get on with mine.'

'Well look, Jack, you are awa wi the fairies!'

'Well,' he says, 'fairies here or fairies there, I've got to get on.'

Wee cotton bag o' oatmeal, a big reckin jug, that was a clay jug full of milk, and his mother's girdle on his shoulder. Away goes Jack to the field. Back he comes.

Here's the Fairy king sitting cross-legged. Oh, he had a good fire going. And all the wee fairies sitting round about. All sitting here and sitting there on top of rocks and things the top of this knowe. And they had a good fire goin!

'Now,' Jack said, 'look, I've to bake a bannock. I'll have to bake it on the girdle.'

'Well, said the Fairy king, 'we want to see it done. And we want to eat it after it's done.'

Jack said to his ownself, 'I hope it poisons you when I do mak it!'

So Jack shook some of the oatmeal into the jug. He stirred it round with a wooden spoon till he got it thick. And he put more meal in till he got it a right thick paste. He got the girdle down and he spread it all on the top of the girdle till he got a good thick bannock made. Then he dried it off with oatmeal and wiped it clean with the bag. And he put it sitting on the top of the fire.

The Fairy king was sitting cross-legged watching the fire. Oh, the smell of this thing cooking was just going to him. He walked over to the corn field, the field beside the wee knowe. And he pulled a corn straw out. He broke the top off it. And he broke the bottom off it. Then he went to the fire and he took out a wee hot coal. He bored seven holes down the corn straw with the coal. And he put it in his mouth.

Jack was sitting cooking this bannock. And the Fairy king started with the corn straw, started playing the jigs and the reels Jack never heard before in his life.

Jack said, 'In the name of God, whaur . . .'

He said, 'I'm the Fairy king!'

'God that I could play like that,' said Jack. 'That's the best music ever I heard.'

'Ye never heard nothing, Jack, ye never heard nothing yet! You got a thing for telling the time?'

'Aye,' said Jack, 'it's half past eight.'

'Well,' he said, 'time you had that bannock made!'

Jack got the bannock made, cooked it bonnie and brown

on each side. Took off his mother's girdle, left it down at the side of the fire, wiped it clean with the bag.

'Noo', said the Fairy king, 'I want you to break it intae as many wee bits as you can.'

'What?' says Jack.

And he says, 'Gie me the first bit!'

Oh, a bonnie bannock it was. It wasn't very round, but it was good. Well made, well het. Jack sat and he spread the wee white bag down. He took the bannock and he broke it into as many wee bits as he could. Wee squares. And the first bit he gave to the Fairy king.

The Fairy king put it in his mouth. He clap-clap, clapped his two hands. And about seventeen or twenty wee men jumped up:

He says, 'Right, boys, bring on the wine!'

Away about twenty of them went. They disappeared behind this rock. And they came out carrying these wee leather bags. Oh, they weren't very big, no any bigger than monkey thimbles, you know, foxgloves. These wee leather bags on their backs. And right – the Fairy king got them all queued up. And the Fairy king gave every one a bit of bannock apiece, and kept the biggest bit for himself.

'Noo,' he said, 'Jack, you're no getting nane. But I'll tell ye, we'll no be too bad to you – we'll gie you a drink o' wine!'

'What?' says Jack, 'fairies drinkin wine? And eatin bannocks? What kind of story am I gaun to tell my mother?'

He said, 'You'll nae tell your mother naething when you go back!'

But anyway, they came bag after bag, bag after bag – they kept carrying bag after bag full of wine from the back of this rock on the knowe. And the Fairy king started to play. And they started to dance, everyone started to dance. There were big ones dancing, wee ones dancing, old ones dancing, young ones dancing. They were all dancing round this knowe.

And Jack, he's lying on his side beside the fire, beside his mother's girdle and he's watching them. He's drinking these wee bags of wine. Till Jack got drunk. Blind miraculous drunk he got and he couldn't drink another drop. Completely drunk out, and the fairies are still going at it. They're dancing and singing and carrying on and carrying wee bags of wine from the back of this rock. As much as they could go till near twelve o'clock in the day, till Jack drunk that many that he couldna drink nae more! He nearly conked out. The Fairy king came over and Jack was lying on his side:

'Jack,' he said, 'you've done your thing well. That was a good bannock!'

And Jack said, 'Aye, that was good wine. It's too good!'

'Here!' said the Fairy king, 'tak a wee sip of my ain private bottle!' And he took out a wee leather bag like that, and he gave Jack one sip.

Jack put it to his mouth and tasted it. He took a good drink out of it, the wee toy leather bag. It was the funniest, best wine that Jack ever tasted in his life. And he no sooner drank it till he fell asleep. Sound asleep he fell.

He must have slept till the sun rose in the middle of the sky. When he wakened he looked at his watch. Twelve o'clock. There was not a soul to be seen.

Everybody was gone. Gone was his girdle. Gone was his mother's bag. Gone was the mark of the fire. Jack sat up on top of the wee knowe. He rubbed his two eyes.

'In the name of God,' he said, 'I must hae slept a while. Did I sleep a while! My mother's wee puckle corn is doin weel now!'

And he looked all around him. His scythe was stuck in the ground. But the corn was cut – the most beautiful cut you ever saw in your life. And it was made into the bonniest wee stooks you ever saw in your life! They were all in line with each other facing to the sun. Jack rubbed his eyes.

He said, 'Was I dreaming? I couldna been dreaming . . . but whaur's my mother's girdle?' He looked all around. 'I couldna get the scythe out of the ground . . . did I really see fairies? But I must have.'

He walked over. He lifted the scythe. It came away in his hand as easy as could be. He put the scythe on his shoulder. He walked back.

'I'll no say much to my mother,' he said. 'I couldna haen my mother's girdle here to the field and kindled a fire to the fairies . . . I must hae cut the corn and fell asleep.'

Jack had nae mind on anything after the Fairy king gave him the drink, you see. He got his scythe on his shoulder and he walked back to the house. Twelve o'clock in the day. And his mother's in the house. The old woman was setting the table for his dinner.

'Come in, Jack,' she said. 'Aye, I see ye're back – ye finished?'

'Aye, Mother,' he said, 'I got finished. I finished the corn. It's all cut and stooked.'

'Aye, good that, laddie. You never ken what kind o' day it's gaunnae be the morn. It could be rain. But once it's stooked it's safe enough.'

'Aye, Mother.'

He never said a word to her, you see. So he sat and his mother gave him his dinner.

He said, 'Mother, there's something funny happened to me today.'

'What was that, Jack?'

He said, 'I never cut your corn.'

'Ah Jack, you never cut the corn? And what are ye daeing back here?'

He said, 'The fairies cut the corn.'

'Fairies cut the corn? Tsst, wha ever seen fairies cutting corn? You and your fairies! You're always gaun on about fairies. Ye're listening too much to your auntie telling fairy stories.'

He says, 'Mother, did I come back here to the house today?'

'No me,' she said, 'I've never seen ye.'

'Ah Mother, come on! Nae makin fun with me – tell me the truth. Did I come back here? To the house? And tak yir girdle, and a jug o' milk and some oatmeal?'

'Laddie, what were ye gaunna dae with that?'

'To bake a bannock, Mother!' he said. 'Sit doon there in your chair and I'm gaunnae tell you a story.' And he tellt her the same story as I'm telling you.

And that's the last o' my wee story.

I mind on my granny telling me this a long, long time ago. My mother's mother, old Bella MacDonald. Oh, she used to tell me, two-three of my brothers and some of the lassies lots of stories. My mother, too, was interested. But Granny wouldn't tell us a story unless she wanted something done. She would say, 'Go for tobacco for me!' or go for something else for her.

You would say, 'Granny, will you tell me a story when I come back?'

'Och,' she'd say, 'I'll tell you a story!'

The Gamekeeper

Many people who heard this story from the person it happened to believed that he'd had a dream, but we'll never know, because it's an old traditional folk tale that's passed down in time. Did he have a dream or didn't he? But he himself told the story the way it's been told to me, by an old man many years ago who had heard it passed down.

This story took place a number of years ago away up in Sutherland. There on a large estate lived a gamekeeper and his name was Angus McPherson. His grandfather had been a gamekeeper before him, his father had been a gamekeeper, it was a family tradition. And Angus was the last remaining one of the McPhersons to be gamekeepers. Angus had a wife called Margaret, a very pleasant woman; and he had a little daughter called Margaret after his wife, and she was in the old university in St Andrews in the Kingdom of Fife. Angus was a pleasant person, he was loved and respected by the people who really knew him.

But at heart Angus was a killer, not a killer of people – oh, he had a great love and respect of people! But he was dedicated to his job for his master the laird to protect his master's wildfowl, for the shooters who would come. He had what they call a gamekeeper's larder, a large board against the fence. And on that board would be all the little creatures he could see that were a menace to his master's game; he killed hedgehogs, he killed squirrels, he killed crows, he killed hawks, he even had a golden eagle, which you're not allowed to touch. He killed foxes, he killed pine martens, he killed every little creature that was a menace, otters. He'd hang them on his board to show his master and show the people that he was doing his work. He had two vicious Labrador dogs.

And on the land where he lived nearby there was a little lake, a freshwater lake a river ran through towards the sea. During the early summer all the salmon would come up and sea trout would come up. He had a little boat in which he would take his master's guests out to do fishing with the fly, and he was an expert on fly fishing himself! If they couldn't get a fish when he took them out in a boat, he would say that he would get one for them.

He was a good man, his wife and him were very happy together. He didn't hurt anybody. The only thing he ever hurt was the little ones, the little creatures who had done him no harm. Till one day the telegraph boy had arrived at his house with his bicycle and he handed Angus a telegram, which they did in these bygone days, a piece of yellow paper.

And he opened it: from his little daughter Margaret from St Andrews. She was coming home for a week's visit, and had been gone for a few months to university. I think she was studying a medical profession of some kind.

And the couple were delighted that their little daughter was coming home. She would be eighteen or twenty. And Margaret began to bustle about the house and prepare:

'What will we make for our tea?'

And Angus said, 'Ach, never mind, sweetheart, I'll just pop down and take the boat out, get a sea . . . a lovely fresh sea trout for our tea. That should be good.'

'Oh,' she said, 'that's a wonderful idea.'

So he took his fishing rod from the cupboard, and a box of flies. He walked down to the little lake. Calm and beautiful it was and a little river running into it running to the sea. He pushed out the little rowboat he'd used many times with his master's guests, pushed it out, laid his fishing rod by his side, rowed out to about the middle of the lake. It was a lake maybe four or five acres. And then, he was just about to pick up his rod and put on a fly when he saw the water breaking a little bit in front of him, he saw the head of an otter coming up, a large otter.

And the first thing that came in his mind: 'Did I no get rid of all youse guys? I thought I'd killed all of you,' he said. 'You're a menace to my master's fishing,' and he saw that the otter had a fish in its mouth.

It began to bite and snap and bite and snap and he forgot about his rod. He watched, and the otter seemed to snap and bite, just snap and bite the fish.

And he saw the fish glinting in the sun. In the distance he could see these strange colours like it wasn't far away. It was like an overgrown goldfish.

And then, as if the otter seemed to get fed up with it, it let it go out of its mouth. The otter sank and disappeared.

The first thought in his mind: 'I'll get you one of these days!'

And then he saw the fish coming towards him. It made its way with its back out of the water towards the boat and it came alongside. For the sake of having a better look he leaned down and caught it in his hands. He lifted it up; it was a fish about four or five pound and he placed it on the backseat of the boat.

He sat there and watched it. He looked at it. It was not gasping like any other fish.

But the most amazing thing that startled him – its two eyes were in the very front like a human being, like you and me. Fish have got an eye each side; they can only see when they turn their head. But this fish had the two eyes, brown eyes . . . . he was startled, amazed. It wasn't gasping but wasn't dead, wasn't hurting in any way. It was so strange. And he sat and looked at it.

The fish was as if it was looking through him, seeing in his very soul and he felt a strange feeling coming over him. He took the fish and lifted it, put it back in the water. It swam away and disappeared. And he sat there for a long time. He never picked up his rod.

He rowed the boat back to the little place where he beached it. He picked up the rod, walked up and put the rod in the cupboard, sat down in his chair by the fire.

And his wife said, 'Did you get a trout, Angus?'

He never spoke.

And she looked at him: 'Angus, what's come over you?' She says, 'You're pale, are you coming down with a chill or something?'

'No,' he said, 'I'll be all right.'

'Wait a moment.' And she went and got him a dram of whisky, says, 'You're coming down with something, a dose of the cold or something, you don't look well at all.'

'I'm all right, Margaret, I'll be fine.'

But she brought him a glass of whisky. She says, 'Did you . . . ?'

'No, 'he says, 'I didn't, I didn't, I didn't do any fishing.'

'I knew there was something wrong with you. You don't look well at all, you look so strange.'

Anyway, he took a glass of whisky and he sat there, but he couldn't get the thought out of his mind of this strange fish he'd seen.

And then a taxi drew up. It was his little daughter Margaret came in. The first thing she saw was her daddy sitting by the fireside, a coal fire, sitting in his favourite armchair by the fire.

She says, 'How are you . . . Daddy, what's come over you?'

'Nothing, my dear,' and he stood up and gave her a hug.

'Daddy,' she says, 'you're trembling. There's something wrong with you.'

'No,' he said, 'my dear, I'm fine. I'm fine.'

And her mother said, 'I've been telling him that all afternoon to go to bed but he won't go.'

But anyway Angus had another dram of whisky.

'I'll make something for supper,' she said.

So they sat there and he seemed all right, but he couldn't get the thought out of his mind. They sat and talked, discussed things about her work and everything else, and after a couple of whiskies he seemed a wee bit better. And then the women carried the dishes into the kitchen.

He sat there by the fireside in his chair and then lo and behold the next thing, slap, there it was – on his knee! A strange fish and this time its mouth was open and its eyes were staring out. He was paralysed with fear. He didn't know what to say.

It sat there. And it spoke:

'Angus McPherson, why do you do it? What have the little ones done to you? Have they ever hurt you in any way? You kill them, you destroy their lives, and you nail them to a board for no reason. I think you should stop before it's too late.' And the fish was gone.

And then he heard his wife and daughter coming in from the kitchen. He looked at his knee and had to hide it with his hands because the knee of his trousers was soaking wet.

Right through. He held it with his hands till it seemed kind of dry.

So that night they talked to him for a long time, but Angus never mentioned to his wife or to his little daughter the experience he had just before they arrived from the kitchen.

But then little Margaret said good night and went to her bedroom and Angus went to his bed with his wife. He lay there all night but he tossed and turned, he could not sleep. His wife was a little upset.

She said, 'Angus, there's something coming wrong with you.'

'No,' he said, 'I'll be fine.' Finally he fell asleep.

Now it was the wife's custom every morning, she would slip out of bed and bring Angus a cup o' tea till he got ready to go to his work. And this morning she brought him a cup of tea as usual. He sat up in bed and she gave him a cup of tea:

'Angus, it's time to get up and go to work, you have your cup of tea.'

He took a couple of sips of tea and left it down, but he still sat there. He said, 'Margaret, I'm no going to work anymore.'

She says, 'What?'

'I'm not going to work anymore, Margaret,' he says. 'I'm not going to work for the laird anymore. I'm going down to the laird today and I'm putting in my notice.'

'But' she said, 'Angus, this is a tied house. We need the house, we need the home.'

He said, 'There're plenty more jobs, there are plenty more homes.'

So she said, 'I knew there was something wrong, I knew there was something coming over you.'

But after nine o'clock he walked down to the office and

put in his notice to the laird. Everyone was upset, asked him why he was leaving.

He said, 'I have reason of my own.'

And he sold the two dogs, he sold his gun. Angus McPherson moved into the village, got a little cottage in the village nearby and became a street sweeper! Sweeping the streets with his little handcart and his brush sweeping. He helped the old ladies across the street, he helped kids across the street (long before the days of lollipop men) crossing to school. He became a well-known figure in the village, loved and respected by everybody. At night-time at half past four when he finally finished he would pack his barrow, hurl it back to the little shed where he kept it. And he said to himself with a smile:

'There'll probably be more caramel papers and crisp papers and things in the street tomorrow thrown by the kids to sweep up.'

But Angus McPherson was happy for the first time in his life. And he stayed in that village till he finally retired.

He met his local friends in the pub and one night after a few drinks he told this story. People listened with interest because they had often wondered, why did he give up his good job as a gamekeeper to become a street sweeper? But Angus McPherson had his own reasons and many people thought it was a dream he had. Maybe it was!

We'll never know, but it's a good story.

Wounded Seal

This silkie story was first told to me a long time ago in Argyll by an old gamekeeper and deer stalker called Peter Munro. I used to go with Peter sometimes when he took out his pony. When he shot a deer out on the hill, a big stag, he would need a help to lift the stag onto the back of the pony. He would come by where I was working and ask the old farmer:

'Can I borrow Duncan for an hour?'

He would pay me half a crown and I always looked forward to this because it was extra money. We were sitting resting one day when I asked him about stories, and this is one he told me.

It all began a long time ago on one of the islands off the north of Scotland. There lived a fisherman and his name was Duncan MacKinnon. And Duncan was a good fisherman. His parents had died and left him a large house, a large piece of land and some money. But Duncan was more of a hunter than a fisherman. For he liked to hunt the seals.

He would kill them on the little island where he lived, take the skins home, stretch them out, salt and stretch them and leave the bodies of the seals lying in the sea to rot. And he preferred this. Now there were no restrictions against killing seals back in that long bygone time, and Duncan was famed as a seal killer. Everybody bought his skins, for they were in great demand.

But there was one thing Duncan MacKinnon would not touch – a young seal – not even a half-grown seal. Whether he thought to himself: 'I'll leave them till they grow bigger and I'll have a bigger skin,' or whether he really felt sorry for the younger seals, he felt some pity because they were young, I don't know. But he never killed a young seal of any kind. He always went for the old ones.

And he used to wait till they were lying sunning themselves on the island not far from where he lived. He only carried a knife, no gun, no stick, just a big long knife. He'd crawl up, get as close to the seal as he could while the seal was sunning itself, dive on the seal and stick the knife in its neck, kill it. Then he would skin it and throw the body of the seal into the sea.

Now through the years he'd collected and sold many skins. Then for some strange reason people stopped buying his skins. And he had a large collection of skins. He was wondering what he was going to do with them. But he still continued to kill the seals and collect them up.

It was near the beginning of wintertime, and it was a terrible stormy night. He was sitting in his house by the peat fire smoking his pipe when he heard a knock on the door. He wondered to himself who could this be? Because he didn't get very many visitors; only when he walked to the village and had a drink in the pub would he have a news with the rest of the folk. Not many people came a-calling as late as this. It was around ten o'clock.

He thought to himself, 'I wonder who this could be.'

He went to the door and he opened it. In this strange dark light in front of the house he saw a tall, dark stranger with a long, dark coat reaching to his feet with his neck buried in the collar of the long, dark, black coat.

The stranger spoke in a kind of Highland accent:

'Are you Duncan MacKinnon? The seal hunter?'

'I am. Can I help you?' said Duncan.

He said, 'Yes, you can. Have you any sealskins for sale?'

'At the moment, I have.'

'Well,' he said, 'I have someone waiting to buy every one from you. Would you sell them to him?'

'Oh well, I have plenty skins to sell. Where is your friend?'

'He didn't come down, he's kind of tired. We walked a long way. He's sitting on the top of the cliff.' Now there was a large, deep, deep cliff not far from where Duncan lived. He said, 'It's not far away.'

Duncan said, 'I know the place well.'

'Well, if you'd like to walk up and have a talk to him I think he'll buy all your skins from you.'

Duncan had never seen this stranger before in his life. And he'd never heard such a strange mixed accent of a voice. It was neither Gaelic nor English. It was inbetween both.

So he says, 'Just a moment, I'll get my coat.'

He got his coat and he came out. By this time the storm had calmed. The stranger said:

'All right, are you ready?'

He said, 'I'm ready.'

'Let's walk then.'

So they walked along the pathway that led to the cliff. And Duncan could barely keep up with the stranger with his long, strange strides he was taking. He could see he was very tall and he looked powerfully built.

He must have been six feet tall, and he was striding on with this long coat. Duncan looked down at his feet in the fading light and he could see he had long, black socks up under the coat. Strong, thick, heavy boots. Duncan wondered where he could have come from?

He said to himself, 'He looks like a rich man. And if his friend is as rich as he looks he'll be able to buy all my skins!' This is what he was looking forward to.

So they walked together, went up the cliff. And the moon was under the clouds and the clouds were passing by. There was a breeze blowing. It was kind of cold, it was kind of dark and kind of misty. They walked up the cliff. Duncan had walked it many times. He'd never actually been at the top, but he knew where it was. So they climbed.

When they came to the top of the cliff it was high – a deep drop nearly five hundred feet into the sea below. And when the tide was full in it was very, very deep.

The stranger stopped. He said:

'Are you there?'

There was no answer.

Duncan stood behind him.

He said louder, 'Are you there? Friend?'

There was no answer.

And then he turned round to Duncan and he said: 'He seems to have wandered off somewhere. I wonder where he can be.' Then he came up as close to the cliff edge as he could. And he said, 'Doesn't it look deep down there? Do you see anything down there? Maybe he's fallen in.'

Duncan came up close to the edge and looked over. Just the moment he did that the stranger put his arm around him – and they dived into the sea! Down and down and down they went with a splash. And then he felt a hand going around his mouth! Down into the deep . . . and down and down they went. And he could see the stranger was a powerful swimmer, for as they went down and down he could feel the stranger's hand holding his mouth, till his lungs were bursting. And he was choking for a breath of air. But down went the stranger. And then he felt his feet turning, touching bottom. The stranger's arm was still around him. And gasping for a breath – he was about to choke for the want of air – when he was led into a passageway under the sea through to the face of the cliff. And he gasped for air – the stranger took his hand away from his mouth. They were in a long tunnel under the cliff.

And he had a strong grip on his arm, he said, 'Duncan MacKinnon, come with me! I want you to meet my friends.'

Duncan wondered, 'What could this be?'

And he half pulled Duncan, half led him through a long, dark tunnel. Then they saw a light ahead. In the light was a great cavern. And all those flares on the walls, flares blazing. Duncan could see that the whole cavern was lit up.

Then to his amazement he looked and saw all these people sitting around on these kind of stone chairs. There were old people, young people, all dressed in black, all looking the same with their brown eyes. They were staring straight at him as he was marched in between the whole group. There were old men, there were young people, there were women sitting with babies wrapped in black cloths on their backs.

But no one said one single word. They just sat and stared. And there was a fire burning in the centre of the cavern. He was led up to the fire.

Then the man spoke: 'I have him.'

Then all the men rose. The women sat still. The men came up and Duncan could see every one's arm held a big long knife!

And he said: 'Oh, my God, I'm going to be killed! What have I done?'

Then the stranger turned round and he pulled down the neck of his coat. Duncan could see he had dark eyebrows, he had dark brown eyes.

And he said, 'Duncan MacKinnon, I have brought you here. You see, you have been killing our people.'

'People?' says Duncan. 'I-I-I've never killed anyone in my life.'

He said, 'You've been killing our people, our seal people. And we have brought you here!'

Duncan thought, 'I'm going to be killed. This is the end for me. Who are these people? Where have they come from?'

And the stranger said, 'Yesterday you did something terrible. You stabbed my father. But he was lucky, he escaped. Now come with me!'

And he led him through a little passage in the cavern. There on a stone bench lay an old man with long grey hair. And his face was pale, his eyes were closed. And stuck in his shoulder was Duncan's big knife! For Duncan had wrestled a seal the day before and the seal was so powerful that he'd escaped with Duncan's knife still in his back.

And the tall stranger said: 'Is that your knife?'

Duncan said, 'Yes, it's my knife.

'Well, that's my father! Come with me!' He led him over.

The old man was lying on his mouth and nose like this, with his head twisted to the side. And he could see that the coat had been split down the back of his neck and there was a great big wound. It was full of pus, and the knife was still stuck in it.

And the tall stranger said to him: 'Duncan MacKinnon, pull out that knife!'

Duncan reached over and he pulled out the knife. He saw that there were pus and blood sticking to the knife.

'Now,' he said, 'that's what you've done to my father. But there's one thing, Duncan MacKinnon, you have never done. That we appreciate a little, but not much – you have never killed any of our children. And for that we are going to give you a chance. I want you to go and kiss that wound that's on my father's shoulder.'

He had no other choice! So Duncan walked over. He reached over – and the smell of the pus of the thing with his nostrils he could feel – the big bloody wound.

'Go on,' said the stranger, 'kiss it!'

And Duncan leaned over for he had no other choice, for the peril of his life – and he kissed the wound of the old man's shoulder – and just like that a strange thing happened. For, as he kissed the wound on the old man's shoulder the old man turned round and his eyes lighted up. And he said:

'Thank you, Duncan!' He sat up. 'Now,' he said, 'Duncan MacKinnon, for what you've done we're going to give you one more chance.'

Not another soul said a word. The old man, he stood up. The look of pain had left his face. His eyes were bright.

They walked back to the fire and the old man heated his hands. He said, 'Bring me a bag!'

And Duncan stood there, he thought he was going to be killed. And one of the young men rushed over and came back with a leather bag. He passed it to the old man. The old man felt it and he weighed it in his hands. And he says:

'Duncan MacKinnon, take this! In the future *do some good to the seals*. Do them no harm!'

And the tall stranger said, 'Then, Duncan MacKinnon, you'd better come with me. And hang on to that bag!'

They never laid a finger on him. All the people stood and stared as he marched away. Not one woman spoke, not one child. Only two people and the old man had spoken.

He led him back through the passage again to the end of the tunnel. And then he put his arm around Duncan's neck once again, hand across his mouth and said:

'Hang on to that bag!'

They swam upwards. And Duncan gasped for breath – just then his head appeared above the surface. And the great powerful stranger swam to the shore, and he pulled Duncan on to the rocks.

'Now,' he said, 'Duncan MacKinnon, remember, *do something good for the seals in the future!*' And he was gone.

Duncan climbed up onto the shore. And he hurried home. He's still hanging on for dear life to this bag! And he could feel that it was heavy. But he went inside, he was soaking wet.

He put the bag on the table. He was trembling with fear. The first thing he did, he rushed and filled himself a glass of whisky. And his hands were shaking. And he drank the whisky. He was lucky to be alive, he thought to himself. And when he had put dry clothes on he sat by the fireside to heat himself for a little while. The fire was still burning brightly. He took the bag made of leather and he emptied it on the table. It was full of hundreds of thousands of gold pieces of all sizes!

Duncan said, 'What has happened to me? This is amazing.' And then he thought to himself, 'I will never touch a seal again as long as I live.'

And he took the Bible, put it on his knee, and he swore to himself in the future he would never touch another seal. Anything he ever did again would be for the good of the seals and for the good of the seals only.

So three days later Duncan sold his house and sold everything he owned. He moved off to another island. There he bought a large piece of land, with an island into it, where seals lived. And he built himself a house on it. He spent the rest of his life protecting those seals, to see that no one would touch them so they could live in peace.

And some people say that that part of the island today is on the Isle of Skye. Duncan MacKinnon lived to be an old man and he never touched another seal as long as he lived.

And that's the end of my story.

Seal House

When I ran away from school at the age of thirteen I was so in love with stories that I thought to myself, because my father and my Aunt Rachel had told me so many fishing stories, there must be a terrible lot among the fishing people. I went west from Furnace to Kintyre and spent two years on the West Coast with the crofting community. I learned so many beautiful stories around by Kintyre, around the lear side up by Kilberry, round by Lochgilphead and down by Bellanoch, finding a wee bit job and searching for stories with a lot of sea and crofting people. But *their* people, some had come from the Western Isles and had brought with them family stories, silkie tales. This one was told to me by an old fisherman, and he said:

'That is a true story.' It happened over a hundred years ago, maybe a little more.

An old crofting man had two sons. He had a small croft, and like all the rest of the crofters he did not have much arable land. He kept a few sheep and a few goats, and only enough animals that could survive on this small piece of land he owned. But his two sons could not survive by working the land, so their father bought them a boat. They would have to make a living from the sea the best they could. Fish for lobsters or crabs, or they could get themselves a net and fish, sell the fish in the market. But they were not the only ones. There were many who turned to the sea to make a living

Now there was no limit against killing seals in these bygone days for their skins. There were thousands and hundreds of seals in all the little rocks and bays along the West Coast. And of course people thought, these seals are taking our food from us. There's too many of them anyway. The fishermen would go out on a cull.

So this one evening a seal cull had been arranged. The fishing was getting poor. There was a big demand for sealskins. They were the finest things for making bagpipe bags in those days. Producers of bagpipes would buy all the sealskins, as many as could be found. So a few friends from neighbouring crofts got together. Six of them. They would go out to Seal Island. Just a barren island where the seals lived. Some men came from three and four miles away for the cull. They got together, just like going to a ceilidh.

For the seals it had been a beautiful sunny day. And the plan for the cull was to go in the evening, when the seals would lie in the late sunshine after feeding all day long. The boat would pull in at one end of the island. The men would creep round the island, two would come from the north, two would come from the east, two would come from the west. They would try and trap the seals in the middle. The seals would be basking on the rocks, enjoying the heat from the stones and the heat from the sun. Seals love sunshine! They would have their bellies full of fish and lie there till they got hungry. Some would be asleep. They would hardly ever hear the boat coming in. Quietly. Of course, if the seals tried to run this way or that once the men were around them there would always be two men to knock them over with their clubs. Beat the brains out of the seals. Kill as many as they could while the other ones escaped into the sea. And maybe that night they would kill a dozen. Now a dozen sealskins shared between six of them would be a good day's wages. So it was arranged. The men had a few drams together. They sat, they talked and waited for the long evening sun.

But not far from Seal Island a businessman a long time ago had built himself a big two-storey house from bricks or stones. But there he lived by himself. No one knew where he came from. Some people said he was a foreigner. But he didn't mix with the local people. He was known as 'the Foreigner'. It was called the Foreigner's House. He'd built this beautiful house on the far shore and a large driveway leading up to it. But this was across from the island, and across the sea loch. After a few years, whatever happened, he seemingly gave up. The Foreigner moved away. Whether he came from Russia or Germany no one actually knew. The Foreigner left the large house. He gave it to no one. No one lived in that house any more. And as the years passed on the house became derelict. The windows got broken with the gales. The doors were unpainted. The Foreigner's House lay vacant for many years.

But these six young men that evening took their boat after they had a good drink, and they rowed out to the island. They knew there were many seals there that night. They came in quietly to Seal Island. And lo and behold there were the seals lying! But the moment they landed on the island every seal vanished. All the seals as if they had been forewarned jumped into the sea. There was not one single seal they could capture or strike that night. And the six of them gathered in the middle of the island and stood there.

They said, 'What's happened? We've never seen this before.'

They stood in a semi-circle, they lighted cigarettes. Some smoked pipes. And then, down at that very moment, even though it had been a beautiful sunny evening, came the mist! Now this island was known for the mist, but it had never come at this time of the year. But within a few moments just as they stood there the whole island was blackened with mist. They had come about two miles from the mainland to this island. And you know, rowing a boat in thick fog or mist is a hard job.

They stood and talked, they talked and talked. And the mist got thicker and thicker and thicker. They said to each other:

'What's gone wrong? What's happened? What's going on here?' They'd never seen this before. There was not a seal in sight. 'Well,' they said, 'we'll have to make our way home to the mainland.'

So, it was a long clinker, built wooden boat. It would hold up to about twelve people. There were three rowing and three sitting at the back. They pulled out into the sea. But the mist was so thick you could barely see your finger before you. It got dark. They had stayed longer on the island than they'd meant to, waiting for the mist to clear. Now darkness came along as well. They didn't know which direction to take. Then they looked across. They saw the lights. So they pulled further out into the sea.

But at that moment they were surrounded by seals! The seals came from all directions. And some of them were around the boat and climbing on the boat. They were pushing the boat, trying to flip to get into the boat. Trying to cowp it the best way they would with these six men in the boat. The men were in a terrible problem.

Now seals as a rule don't get together, only once in a year has anyone ever seen a seal gathering. Seals like to keep by themselves. But this was the largest collection of seals the men had ever seen in all their lives. They nearly overpowered the boat. The men of course got their oars and stopped rowing, started punching the seals. These seals were going to cowp the boat, put them in the sea a long way from the mainland!

But then up from behind the boat came an old bull seal. And the men could see that he was very old. He had put his flippers across the boat. The weight of him was pushing the boat down. One of the men took his oar and he hit the old seal in the mouth, and he knocked all his teeth out. He saw the blood. It disappeared in the sea. And then every seal was gone.

So they rowed around in circles and circles in the dark in the fog. Then they saw a light again.

'Let's make for the light, boys!' they cried.

So they rowed for the light. They beached the boat. But they were far away from the village. Where were the lights coming from? The old Foreigner's House!

They said, 'It must be somebody's taken over the house. Maybe they'll give us shelter. Maybe they'll give us a dram. We'll wait till daylight.'

So they made their way up the beach to the old Foreigner's House that had been derelict for many years. But when they landed there the house was in a lunary of lights! The whole house was lighted. So they knocked on the door and the door opened.

This tall dark man with a long dark coat said: 'Hello, come on in! Make yourselves at home!'

They all came in, one by one, six of them. There was a table. There were bottles of drink, liquid laid in the middle of the table. And all those people around against the wall. Strangers they had never seen. But everyone was dressed the same way. Long dark coats. There were old people, young people. There were teenagers, young women, there were old women. There must have been over a hundred of them. And they were all sitting around the room. Of course, these fishermen had never seen the likes of this before in their lives. They lined up against the wall.

So the spokesman for the whole crowd said: 'Be seated! Welcome, gentlemen, to our home. But we cannot do anything till Grandfather comes. You can enjoy yourselves. You can have as much to drink as you like, but we'll have to wait on Grandfather.'

These men were terrified. They'd never seen these strange people before. No one was recognisable; everyone was looking very, very strange. The women with these burning brown eyes. These fishermen were afraid. Some of the people were standing, some were sitting, some sitting around the table.

Then they said: 'Gentlemen, we'd like to give you something to drink, but we'll have to wait on Grandfather.'

They sat there for a few minutes. They didn't know what to do. They knew in their own minds this was the Foreigner's House. It had been derelict for many years. Where did these people come from? They were not local villagers. They were not crofters.

And there was a stair leading down in the middle of the house. Down the stair comes an old man with a long grey beard.

They all cried: 'Granddad, Grandfather, come here! We've someone to show you. We have something to show you.'

And these six fishermen were lined against the wall. And Grandfather came down. They could see that his beard was tainted red with blood. And when he came to the middle of the room he looked round:

'Oh,' he said, 'these are the ones.' And he opened his mouth, and all his front teeth were knocked out! His gums were red with blood. He says, 'Kill them!'

Every one around the room drew their knives. Long knives from under their coats, from under their jackets, from anywhere. And these fishermen, they stood terrified. The one who was near the door put his back against it. He opened the door carefully with his hand.

He said, 'Boys, let's go! Run for your lives!'

And one after one they ran out of that house. There were screams and shouts. But no one followed them. They ran to their boat. They jumped in and they rowed back. By this time the mist had cleared. They knew where they were going – home!

These men were terrified as they rowed that boat home that night across the sea loch from the Foreigner's House. And when they landed on the beach and pulled the boat up they stood together. They said:

'What happened? Who were those people?'

'Let's go home tonight,' one said. 'We'll find out tomorrow.'

So they all split up and went to their homes. But they could not rest. Some sat, some drank, some fell asleep. Some went home to their old wives, some did not go. But the next morning they made a pact they would find the truth. When the sun was shining there was nothing to be afraid of.

Six of them with guns rowed back across the sea loch to the Foreigner's House. Pulled the boat on the beach up on the shore, with shot guns and everything else they marched up! Who were these foreigners who were in the old house? They were going to find the truth. Who terrified them, nearly caused them their deaths?

But when they walked up to the house the door was hanging on its hinges. The windows were full of cobwebs. The floor was full of dust. There was no one there. They searched the house up and they searched house down. And the spokesman of the group, an old crofting man said:

'Boys, look, I'll tell you something; look, we have come in contact with the *seal people*. I think it would be better if we leave these people alone. Because my grandmother used to tell me many many stories. I think we have killed too many seals.' And from that day on not another one of these six people ever killed another seal for their skins.

And that's the end of my story.

The Cull

Many of these beautiful stories remain untold. I'm only sorry for one thing: I wish I had have collected a lot more than I ever did, which is two-three hundred seal stories. Anyway, one I really love and respect is this story about Angus Cameron. Now you have to get government permission today to have a cull.

So my story begins on a little island many years ago, and the local fishermen were getting problems like they always do with the seals. Because these fishermen in the little island didn't have trawlers; they were inshore fishermen and set their nets along the coast in different places. Most of them only had little boats they'd row out and spread their nets from off the rowing boat.

But they managed to make a living apart from the trouble they had with the seals coming in . . . a big hole in the net takes a lot of patience and time to mend and it kind of annoyed the people of the village, especially the fishermen. They were always complaining. Even to the local minister in the village they complained.

So, they put it to Alasdair, the gamekeeper of the village, well respected, retired and a crack shot with a rifle. So he said, as a spokesman, they would meet in the church and have a talk. Maybe they could have a cull, kill off some of the seals to protect the people's nets. The word spread in the village, and of course the men in the village gathered, maybe some of the women too.

He explained that they'd have to cull some of the seals because the island was a bay and a group of rocks. In the evening the seals would come in, lie on the rocks, bask in the evening because the seals disna stay in the water overnight. He said:

'We'd love to kill some, shoot some of the seals to protect the fishermen against their livelihood, and if we could kill a few it would always help.'

So they put it to vote in the church hall and voted by about twenty to one, they were going to have their cull. The gamekeeper said to them:

'Collect your guns, whatever gun you have.'

He had a repeating rifle, the only one who had a decent gun in the whole island. And some of the men collected old single barrel shotguns. With a few bottles of whisky they made their way.

Now, in the village, there visited a young man called Angus Cameron. Angus Cameron was very good-looking, tall with dark hair, brown eyes. He lived in a little cottage by the sea away at the end of the island with his mother, who was a cripple and very rarely appeared in the village. Angus would always bring whatever his mother needed.

But some people said they used to see her with a couple of walking sticks walking among the seals . . . that's all the glimpse they got of her. The people said:

'Oh, she never appeared in the village, she had lost her husband at sea drowned off a boat. He was never found.'

But Angus Cameron was a lovely man and always wore this big long coat coming to his ankles. People didn't understand it. And some of the kids in the village would come up, pat the coat to feel the soft warmness. All the young women loved him, even some of the married women had a great respect for him. He had no time for any of them. But he was kind and gentle.

And the thing was, if anybody got in trouble with a boat capsized or something Angus was always there! He had saved many lives in the village. People loved and respected him for it. He was the finest swimmer in the whole island. He had saved many children's lives, was a great powerful swimmer. If kids were out in a boat and it capsized he would be there! If men got in trouble with a boat he would seem to appear from nowhere. And he did appear that night.

So, they all gathered with their guns they could get, about a dozen guns among them. The gamekeeper spokesman, a couple of bottles of whisky with them and they made their way down towards the beach to the rocks below. Mostly the men in the village and the young men who wanted a shot to fire a gun, about twenty of them. Angus Cameron went with them. But no gun.

So they sat there waiting. The whisky passed along. Angus took no drink, he didn't drink. He was loved and respected but he didn't mingle with the people. But they sat and they waited and the whisky passed by. They talked, they waited and they talked and they waited. They waited. It was a summer's evening.

But nobody had noticed when Angus Cameron had disappeared. He had gone for some reason.

Alasdair said, 'Maybe he's away back to his mother. Maybe she needs him, the old crippled woman.'

So they waited. Twelve o'clock. No seals came in. One o'clock, two o'clock. By three o'clock the whisky was finished. They had nothing to drink but they were still waiting for the seals.

But at five o'clock the gamekeeper said, 'I doubt, boys, they are not coming in. Something must have disturbed the seals tonight, they're not coming in. There's no use awaiting any longer.'

And they were just about to depart for their homes after a long night sitting on the rocks, some of them stiff and tired, when they looked about a hundred yards out and saw the head of a seal coming towards them.

And the gamekeeper said, 'Well, there's one coming in anyway! We'll get that bugger.'

He laid his repeating rifle on the rock and they watched. He fired, hit the seal. And it floated on the top of the water. He told two-three of the young men to take a boat and go out, bring in the seal.

'At least we'll get his skin,' he says, 'it'll be one we can hang up.'

So they rowed out the boat. But they didn't find the body of a seal; they found the body of young Angus Cameron floating on the sea – with a bullet hole through his forehead. So they brought him in and everybody was really upset, really upset. They had no option but to carry him back to the village, to the church hall, and they carried him back.

Everyone in the village turned up. The person who they had respected and liked so much was dead. He was killed. But everyone there swore it was a seal! It was not Angus Cameron the gamekeeper had shot; he had nothing to do with it, he had only shot a seal.

So they had no option but to carry him down to the cottage of his mother, down to the little cottage away at the shoreside. They put him on a stretcher and half a dozen of the people, some of the women were weeping, carried him down. They carried the corpse of young Angus down to his mother and opened the door of the little cottage.

There were moss and fog growing on the carpet, moss in the fireplace – the fire had never been kindled for years. They went in to the bedroom. There were fog and mosses growing on the bed. And the rain was dripping through the ceiling. Nobody had lived in that house for many, many years.

So they had no option; they carried Angus's body back to the church and he lay there for three days in the village while people mourned for the loss of their friend.

And finally everyone of the village gathered. He was buried in the little churchyard behind the church. The minister gave a sermon. Everybody contributed for a stone for Angus Cameron's grave, because he had saved the lives of some of the children.

And someone in the village, a man who might have been jealous of Angus Cameron, came in some night when no one was around. Under the name of Angus Cameron he chiselled SILKIE MAN with a hammer and chisel on the gravestone.

And if you were there tomorrow you could see it for yourself.

That story was told to me personally by an old fisherman a long time ago.

Blind Angus

Now this story is very old, perhaps the oldest silkie tale I know. There's no point in me telling you where the story actually came from because we don't really know. Many people have different versions of the same story. I could say one place, and people lay claim to it in another. But the story as I know it began in the Western Isles a long time ago.

It was all because of a cattle dealer called Angus Maclean. Now Angus bought cattle from the local farmers and he kept them for a while, because he had a small croft. He didn't keep any cattle of his own. But he fattened those he bought in, and then sold them to people who wanted to buy them. Now, he would take a few cattle to the market and there he would sell them. He bought all the lean cattle he could find. He was known as Angus Maclean the Cattle Dealer.

To some people Angus was a bit of a rogue because he tried to cheat – well, he was a dealer! Cattle dealers try their best to survive in their own right. Some people loved him, some respected him. Some said he was a rogue, some said he was a hero. But Angus was not only a cattle dealer.

When people used to kill cattle for their own domestic purposes in the Western Isles Angus would buy the skins of the cattle. Because people who needed a bit of meat to survive would kill an animal on their own. It was legal to do that on the Western Isles, to kill a beast if you'd reared it up. Like a shepherd killing a sheep. And of course Angus would buy the skin, take it home, stretch and dry it. But not only the skins of domestic animals did Angus buy; he also bought the skins of seals.

Now people who had no cattle of their own made a living from killing seals, salting the skins and selling them. Sealskins were used for many purposes. Bagpipe makers would buy sealskins for making their bags. And of course Angus was famed for buying sealskins!

Angus went to the local cattle market one morning and he had a fine cattle beast that he had bought from somebody. He had kept it for a few weeks, maybe ten or twelve. But he had fattened it up. He took it to the market and knew he would sell it for a good price because it was fat. Maybe a local butcher would buy it.

But as he walked into the market of the small village the first person he met was a tall dark man dressed in black wearing a long dark cloak. He walked up to Angus and said:

'That's a fine beast you have there.'

Angus said, 'Well, it's for sale, you know, and I am a cattle dealer. I don't only deal in cattle; I also deal in hides. If you want, if you have any use for hides, skins or anything, I deal in sheepskins, in cattleskins and sealskins!'

'Oh I see,' said the tall dark man dressed in a long, dark cloak. 'You also deal in sealskins, do you?'

He said, 'Yes.'

'And have you many at home?'

'Well,' Angus said, 'well there's a certain fellow who kills a few seals and he gives me the skins. I salt and stretch them, and sell to the local people who need them. Would you be interested in the sealskins?'

The man said, 'No, not really. I'm more interested in this cattle beast you have.'

And Angus said, 'Well, would you like to buy her?'

The tall dark man said, 'Of course, I would like to buy her! But you see I have a problem.'

Angus said, 'Well, what's your problem?'

He said, 'I would like to buy your cattle beast. But you see, I would like you to take her out to the island, the little island out there.'

'That little island?' says Angus.

Now beside the village where the people were selling in the market there was a little island in the bay, about a mile out. But it was uninhabited. Nobody was on the island. And Angus thought this strange.

He said, 'You mean Lir Isle?'

He said, 'Would you like to go out?'

Angus thought this was very interesting. He said, 'Yes.'

The man asked, 'What is your name?'

'My name is Angus Maclean.'

'Well, Angus, I'll pay you well for that cattle beast because it's nice, if you would take it out to Lir Isle for me.'

But Angus said, 'What do you do out on Lir Isle? There's nothing out there. No habitation of any kind. There's not even a building or a tree.'

'That's my problem. But I'll tell you, Angus, if you're willing to sell your beast to me, and if you could hire yourself a boat and row that beast out . . .'

Now the custom was on the Western Isles, if you had to take a beast to an island, you put a rope on it and you put it behind the little rowing boat. You rowed and the beast swam behind the boat. That's the way they transported cattle a long time ago.

He said: 'I'll pay you in guineas. Gold guineas. What would you be wanting for your beast?'

'Well, I would like about ten guineas for her.'

'Ten guineas?' said the tall dark man. 'That's reasonable. But I'll tell you what I'll do with you: I'll give you twenty gold guineas if you will take her out to the Lir Isle for me and put her on the island.'

But Angus said, 'There's nothing out there! There's not even grain for a beast.'

And the man said, 'That's my problem! Could you hire yourself a rowing boat? And you and I will row the beast out to the island. Deliver it there and I will pay you twenty gold guineas for your beast!'

'Done, sir!'

So Angus had an old friend he knew he could borrow a boat from. Now he never got the length of the market; he led it down the causeway to the beach. He talked to an old friend of his who had a rowing boat. He explained the purpose. And he said:

'Old man, I'll give you a guinea for a loan of your boat to take her to the wee island.'

And the old man, who knew Angus well, said: 'That is fine, Angus, there's no problem. You can borrow the boat. I'm not using it.'

So Angus and the tall dark man went in the boat. They took the cattle beast behind on the rope. Now Angus said:

'You'll have to row the boat.'

'Oh,' the tall dark stranger said, 'I'll row the boat, no bother. It's no problem to me if you'll keep the animal behind the boat. And as I row just make it swim to the island.' It wasn't far out. 'But,' he says, 'there's something I must do before we go out, Angus – I must blindfold you.'

'Blindfold me? What do you want to blindfold me for?'

He said, 'Look, it's no problem, Angus, I won't hurt you. All I want you to do . . .' and he took from his pocket a black handkerchief. 'Angus, all I want you to to do is tie this across your eyes.'

'What do you want that across my eyes for? I'm leading the beast. You'll be rowing.'

'Angus, when we land on the island I don't want you to see what's there.'

Angus said, 'There's nothing to see! Why do you want me to put a handkerchief across my eyes?'

'Angus, I'm telling you, I want you to put this across your eyes! It'll no hurt you. And I'll pay you well. In fact, I'll give you another extra five gold guineas if you put the handkerchief around your eyes!'

'Well,' Angus said, 'there's no problem.'

'You don't need to help me beach the boat. We'll take care of it.'

'*We'll take care of it*?' Angus said.

'Oh, we'll take care of it.'

But Angus said, 'It's only you . . . and I don't see why you're going to take this animal to an island to live on its own. There's nothing out there but rocks and stones.'

The tall stranger said, 'Angus, it's my problem, not yours! I'm paying you well.'

'Well,' Angus said, 'if that's the way you want it that's the way it will be!'

So Angus got in the back of the boat, the big cow on the rope. And the stranger got in the front. But before he went in the front of the oars he took the black handkerchief and tied it around Angus' eyes. And tied it behind his neck. He took the oars and he began to row, Angus with the rope behind the boat with the cattle beast. He rowed out to the island.

And of course the cow once it got into the water began to swim. Cows can swim very well. And he rowed the boat very gently out to the little Lir Isle. The cow went plod, plod,

plod behind the boat. And the man beached the boat. The tide was out and there was a little strand.

Then the stranger got out of the boat and walked around, took the rope from Angus' hand. He said:

'Thank you, Angus,' and he led the beast up the beach.

But the moment the animal was away Angus put his hands up and took the handkerchief from his eyes. And he looked. Angus stared in amazement. For the island was full of people! There were dozens – old men, young and old people.

They rushed forward to the beast. An old man with a grey beard rushed forward. And within minutes they took the beast and cowped it on its back. A dozen of them – they cut its throat. And in minutes they killed it and butchered it on the island.

Angus was amazed! He pulled up the hankie, back over his eyes because he couldn't . . . he never saw a beast butchered so quickly in all his life. He stood there with the handkerchief over his eyes. Where did all these people come from? Angus hadn't a clue. Within minutes they had killed, butchered and quartered an animal in front of his eyes on an island where there was no one!

In minutes the tall black man, dark stranger, came back once again. He said:

'It's all right, Angus. It's fine now. Let's row back to the mainland.'

And he turned the boat, rowed back again. Angus pulled the handkerchief down. They beached the boat on the mainland. The man took a purse from his pocket, he counted out twenty-five gold guineas:

'There you are, Angus,' he said, 'and thank you.' He walked away.

Angus stood there. Now he had the money in his hand.

More money than he'd ever had for a long time. Twenty-five guineas.

He said, 'What in the world had happened? What was going on out there on that island?'

But then he went back home to his wife. He never said a word to her. But deep in his mind he was still thinking about these things that happened on the island. He swore he saw people butcher that animal on that island. But nobody was there!

But anyway, a week was to pass. Angus bought another lean old animal. He had many. He fattened him up in his little croft. Two weeks later it was market time again. Angus picked the fattest beast he could find among his animals. He'd sell another one in the market.

And he walked down to the local village once again with another beast. As he walked into the village there were many farmers around and villagers around, people doing their local business.

As he walked the beast up, up comes the man once again! The same man Angus had met before:

'Hello, Angus,' he said.

'Oh hello,' said Angus, 'hello!'

'That's another fine beast you have.'

'Aye,' Angus said, 'she's not bad. She's put the weight on. She's fat and full. I think I'll sell her well.'

He said, 'Angus, would you sell her to me?'

Angus says, 'No, no way I'm going to sell another beast to you!'

'And why, Angus, are you not going to sell another beast to me? What's the problem? Didn't I pay you well for the last one?'

Angus said, 'You paid me well. You made me row out to the island. And you butchered that beast in front of my eyes! I never saw an animal killed so fast in all . . .'

'O,' he said, 'Angus, so you did – *didn't you see*?'

Angus said, 'I did see. I saw things I never saw in all my life! That island was bare. There was no one there. And I saw people there. I saw an animal butchered in front of my eyes like I've never seen an animal butchered before in all my life!'

'Oh, I see,' said the stranger. 'Well, Angus, you will never see anything again as long as you live!'

And he took his fingers *like that* – snapped his fingers in front of Angus' eyes. And Angus felt something like sand or dust going into his eyes. He closed his eyes. It hurt for a few moments. And Angus looked, but Angus could not see. Angus was blind!

Of course the stranger walked away. But for Angus, he never saw again. He became known as Blind Angus the Cattle Dealer.

But Angus told that story to many people. No one ever believed him. So you've heard the story from me. And probably you won't believe it.

But that is a true story, what happened to Angus the Cattle Dealer a long time ago.

Seal Brother

When I was thirteen I spent some time in Kilberry, between Ardrishaig and Tarbert, with an old rabbit-catcher called Angus MacNeil. I used to walk with him, carry his snares on my back and his rabbits from the hill. He killed and trapped rabbits for a living. And one evening by the fireside I said:

'Angus, do you have any stories, any about the seal people?'

'Well, Duncan, I'll tell you a true story,' he said, 'that happened a long time ago. Now it's a very old story and it was told to me in Gaelic by my grandmother.'

If you were to travel to the West Coast of Scotland, there beside a little village is a graveyard, and in there is a little tombstone shaped like a heart. On that tombstone are four words that say TO MALCOLM AND MARY. People have often wondered why it doesn't say anything else, no dates of birth or anything, just the four words. In bygone days the path leading to the graveyard was just earthen and during the cold and rainy days when people visited the graveyard the path got very wet. Sometimes it turned to mud. If you were to visit that little graveyard today you would find the path leading to that heart-shaped stone is gravel. But in bygone days it was just a muddy little road.

My story takes you back more than a hundred years to a crofting family who lived by the shoreside not far from the village. The man's name was Donald MacDougall and his wife's name was Margaret. Now Donald and Margaret were very happy. They kept a few animals. But Donald's main thing was fishing; where he spent most of his time while Margaret took care of the little stock they had, maybe a few goats or a few sheep, and hens and ducks of course.

But it was the happiest family anyone could ever think of. The reason was, they had two children, twins. The boy's name was Malcolm and the girl's name was Mary. They were born on the very first day of March, a month beginning with 'M'. This was how Malcolm and Mary got their names.

And of course the children attended the local village school. But these children, being twins, were devoted to each other. Not like children you have today, as Angus would tell you. These children really loved each other, more than anything else in the world. And Mary helped her mother and Malcolm helped his father. There was nothing these children would not do for their parents. The parents loved them dearly.

During the mealtimes if there was a little extra food left over, Mary would say, 'Oh, give it to Malcolm!' Malcolm would say, 'No, give it to Mary!' But they never argued, they never fought. Then at the weekends they spent most of their time on the little island not far from where they lived in the little croft.

They would ramble along the beach, play all day long and their parents knew they were quite safe. They were free from all the wide world and were so happy. At night-time they wandered home, their cheeks rosy with the fresh air. Of course they'd have their meal and sit down there. And Father would tell them stories and Mary would tidy up the kitchen, help her mother.

But when Malcolm and Mary were on the island, they were completely devoted to each other. Sitting on the beach together Malcolm would hang his legs over the rock. He was a powerful swimmer from the age of five. Malcolm could swim like a fish! But there was one thing that annoyed Mary – it didn't really annoy her, but she used to torment Malcolm about it: Malcolm was born with an enlarged toe on his right foot. And she would make fun of the toe. Of course, he didn't take it too seriously.

But when he hung his legs over the rock before he went off swimming she would say: 'Malcolm, that's a terrible looking toe you've got.'

'Well, Mary, I can't help it. My parents gave it to me, I'll just have to live with it.' She tormented him but she loved her brother dearly.

Now Malcolm's obsession was swimming. And of course on that island where they played were many many seals. And many's a long evening these children would sit there among the seals. The seals were so used to the children they didn't pay much attention to them. Malcolm would dive in among the seals and he would swim. Mary would say:

'Malcolm, if you don't stop it you'll turn into a seal!' He would come out and sit on the rock and say:

'Mary, that's the only ambition I have. I love these creatures! I wish I could be one of them. Look how they can swim, look how they can dive! Where do they go to?' These children loved the seals and of course the seals paid them no attention.

The children grew up and they went to the same little school in the village. But time passed by, and both of them left school at the same age of fourteen. And when they finished they came back to work with their parents. Malcolm went to sea with his daddy. He was good with a boat and could do anything. The parents had very little to do, because now the children were teenaged they were a wonderful help.

But one evening Donald MacDougall said to his son: 'I think we'll go out tonight and do a bit of fishing,' because it was a beautiful evening.

Mary filled a basket with all the things they would use, bait and hooks, and saw that her brother had everything he needed. Malcolm could row a boat as good as his daddy. And they didn't have any nets. It was all hand lines they fished with. Mary said goodbye to her brother and her daddy and off they went fishing.

Young Malcolm was rowing. But they went further than they usually went because the fishing that night was really good. They went out for cod and anything else they could catch; they would dry their fish, hang them up for the winter. But the weather began to change.

Donald says to Malcolm, 'Malcolm, my son, I think we've gone a little farther than we should tonight. I think we should turn.' Being a fisherman he knew the weather.

But then lo and behold they were caught in a storm. The most severe storm that ever happened blew up at that particular time. And of course there were Mary and her mother at home thinking:

'Oh, they're caught in the storm. What will happen to them? I hope they'll be safe enough.'

And they were out at the front of the house looking at the beach. Mary was watching for her brother and her daddy coming home.

But the storm got so severe, so terribly wicked the boat overturned. Donald MacDougall had no fear for his son because he was a great swimmer. He says to him:

'Malcolm, swim for your life! Make for the shore. Forget the boat, forget everything. Let's save ourselves.'

And Donald MacDougall was a great swimmer himself, being a seaman. And he swam. The terrible storm blew. Donald MacDougall swam to the beach. When he came into the beach he stood up and looked all around. There was no sign of his son. His son was gone . . . his heart was broken! There was his wife Margaret and his daughter to meet him.

'And where is Malcolm? Is he not with you?' Malcolm was gone.

They searched the next day. And they searched far and wide. But Malcolm never turned up. He was lost at sea. Now they took a search party with many boats; because word spread through the little village. They searched for his body, but he never was found. A week passed. Two weeks passed. And then a strange thing began to happen to Mary; she completely changed.

She would sit there, would not talk to her parents. She would not look at them. She would not eat. She would pick at her food. She lost weight. She would not go to the village. All she would do was walk along the beach when she had spare time, staring into the sea. And of course her parents were very worried about her. Their hearts were broken for their little son but they knew that he was gone. There was no chance they would ever find him because two weeks had passed. His body never was found. As for Mary, she became a changed girl. She crawled into her shell. She never helped her mother. She never talked to her father. She just sat around all day long staring at the floor. When she walked alone she would sit on the island staring out to sea. The truth was, her heart was completely broken.

She could not go on with her life without her little brother whom she loved so dearly. But the days were to pass into weeks, the weeks were to pass into months. Her mother would go to the village. Daddy found his boat, and he was still going out fishing. But a big change had come over the family. Mary had become so much drawn into herself that she was completely lost to her parents. This upset them very much. Sometimes the parents would argue with each other during the night, which they had never done in their lives, and Mary would hear them. And she would lie there in her bed, rise in the morning, pick at her little bit of food and then be gone.

But the years passed by and this was the way she lived. She never went to the village. When her mother went to the shop she just stayed at home. She got so indrawn to herself she was just completely lost. But two years were to pass, two long years. Her parents thought they would bring in a doctor or psychiatrist or something.

But Mary said, 'No, I don't want anything to do with them. Just leave me alone, leave me alone! Don't talk to me.' Till one day.

She took a walk along the beach. The tide was out. She walked the beach with her hair straying behind her, staring into the sea. The tide was full out, the gulls were crying. She walked where she had walked many times before with her little brother. By this time she was sixteen years old. The beach was very clear, the sand was very soft along it. But further along, about a mile along the beach, the sand gave way to a lot of rocks. And then a cliff. In there was a cave where Mary had played many times with her little brother Malcolm. But she never visited it anymore.

Then walking along the beach this evening she saw a strange thing in the sand. She saw marks coming out, as if a seal had come up onto the sand, soft sand. Then she stopped. When she saw the marks of the flippers in the sand she knew what it was – a seal had come out – but then there was a terrible change. The flipper marks gave way to foot marks, footprints.

She followed the foot prints. But there was something strange about them as she looked. She followed them, as they were quite plain in the soft sand. And just for curiosity she counted – one, two, three, four. On the right foot there were only four toes. Then she counted the left foot. And she saw one, two, three, four, five. She followed the foot prints gradually along the beach.

She said, 'I wonder what this could be?'

And she felt excitement in her heart. Something strange was taking place. Then she walked along the shore and along the shore. Then the prints stopped because they came to rocks. But she still saw the wet marks on the rocks so she followed. And she climbed up over the rocks. Then she said:

'I'll go to the cave.'

Something told her to go to the cave. When she went in she was in for the biggest surprise of her life. For sitting in the cave was a young man. She looked and she saw, she stared. And she ran in. He stood up. He threw his arms around her.

He says, 'Mary, my sister!'

'Malcolm, Malcolm,' she cried as the tears were streaming down her cheeks. 'You've come home. You've come back to me.'

'Yes, sister,' he says, 'I've come back to you. But not for very long.'

'O Malcolm, Malcolm, where have you been all these years? Where have you been?'

So he threw his arms around her and kissed her. And he said:

'Sister, sit you down here.'

She says, 'You broke my heart. And you broke my parents' hearts. Why didn't you come home?'

'Mary, my dear sister, I couldn't come home.'

'Why didn't you come home? Why have you done this to me?'

He said, 'I had no other choice.'

'Tell me,' she said, 'why is it you have done this to me?'

He said, 'I'll tell you. You remember that night I was caught in the storm with my daddy? And our boat capsized? Well, something happened to me. I seemed to get paralysed. I could not swim. And then, I felt something come and catch me and put her arms around me . . . and she swam with me. Took me to the bottom of the sea. There she led me into a great passage. And there in a great cavern were all those people. You know how much I wanted to be a seal, Mary? How much I enjoyed the love of the seal people? Well, I became one of them!'

And then she stood and looked: 'But, Malcolm, you're so tall. You're so fit!'

He had grown tall, he had grown stout. And his dark hair was streaming down his back. And she looked at his hands. He put his hands around hers, and she saw that in between his fingers were like a duck's foot, with webbed fingers. Then she looked at his foot.

She said, 'Malcolm, what's happened to you? Look at your foot!' For his big toe was gone.

'Well,' he said, 'Mary, my sister, you didn't like it very much.'

But she said, 'Why, Malcolm, why did you lose it?'

'Well, I'll tell you; when the seal people rescued me and you know I love to be with them, I had to give them something of myself – before I became one of them. And I knew you hated my big toe. So I gave them my toe, the only thing you didn't like about me.'

But she says, 'Malcolm, I didn't mean it, I didn't mean it!'

He says, 'It didn't hurt. They took it off. It didn't hurt! I feel fine without it.'

'Malcolm, come home! Mummy and Daddy are dying to see you.'

'No, my dear, I can't come home to Mummy and Daddy tonight, or any other night. And I want you to make me a promise. You will never tell that you've seen me. Promise me right here and now you'll never tell you've seen me!'

She says, 'Malcolm, I promise. Will I see you again?'

He says, 'Mary, you'll see me many many times. But you must never, never tell my parents! Because, you see, I'm happy. This is the life I want. Now, Mary, I must bid you goodbye. But I'll see you again. You know where to find me here.'

And then they walked to the sea. He bade her good-bye and dived in. But she stood there and watched. Sometimes when they were kids he would dive under the sea and he'd be gone for many minutes. She'd thought he was drowned. But this time she waited a few moments, and she thought he was not going to come up. But she looked – about ten yards out up came the head of a great big seal. It shook its head, and then was gone. This was the happiest moment of Mary's life! She was completely transformed. Gone was the thought, gone was the worry, gone was everything.

She hurried back, but she knew she would never tell her parents. When she walked into the house her mummy and daddy were sad, just sitting, and she was singing to herself. And her cheeks were rosy.

Her parents looked . . . a strange thing had happened to Mary. She was singing! She was happy. Her face was flushed. She was standing straight. Her eyes were bright! The parents looked and said:

'Mary has become a transformed girl all together!'

She said, 'Mummy, is the tea ready? Are you needing anything?'

This had never happened for two years. From that moment on Mary became a changed girl. She was back to her natural self. She could not do enough for her parents. She helped them in every way. The last two years had gone into the distance. Now she was sixteen years old. Once again she was happy. She sang at her work as she helped her mother and as she helped her father. She went to the village, talked to everyone. This of course made the parents very happy.

The thought of Malcolm was still in their minds. But seeing Mary like this changed everything for them. Their life began to renew itself. So life like that went on for many, many years. Mary would go off on her long trips along the beach at night time. Her mummy and daddy would say:

'She's off walking along the shore. She enjoys it.' But they looked when she came home.

Every time she came back from her walks on the beach she was brighter, more happy, more handsome-looking, more kind, more willing to help her parents. She helped her daddy in the fishing. She helped her mummy. But she always had those long walks. Now she would go to the village. She would go shopping for her mother. She would go to church with her parents. And by this time she was twenty years old. Another four years had passed by. Mary was the happiest girl in the whole place!

She talked to everyone. She went to the dances. And many young men tried to woo Mary. But no way! She would not look at one single soul. Mary became the happiest young woman in the whole village. And people talked and spoke but no one said an angry word against Mary. They often wondered why she never married. Because she was handsome, she was beautiful, she was kind. And she only had one friend whom she really respected more than anyone else – that was the local minister.

By this time Mary was thirty years old. And she still continued the same way of life. Naturally her parents were growing older and now they were getting up in years Mary completely ruled the little croft. Her daddy stopped fishing. But Mary did fishing of her own. She brought enough back. She could handle a boat. She could do anything. She took care of the stock, did everything for them. And the parents depended on Mary. She would still go for her long walks in the evening. And she'd be gone for hours. Her mummy and daddy could not wait till they heard the click of the door. It was a little latch that opened the door.

In the evening when she came back Mary was smiling and happy. They never questioned her. But they knew wherever she went she was finding happiness. She was finding something that really made her happy.

But unknown to them Mary was visiting the cave on the cliff side. And there she spent most of her time with her brother. They had many long talks together. And he told her many wonderful things.

He told her about his life among the seal people. He told her how they transformed and became seal people down there. And how they walked on the land, how no one could recognize a seal person; sometimes they walked in the village and saw the people going to church but they always returned to the sea.

And of course Mary knew all this. But unknown to her parents she had a little red book at home, and she wrote down every single thing her brother had told her in this little diary. And this was the secret of hers. She had it hidden in her little room, her bedroom.

As I told you, she had one special friend ten years younger than her, the local minister. He was only twenty. He took to the ministry when he was very young. And he lived with his parents. Even though he was a very young minister he lectured in the church on Sunday. Sometimes he would come for a visit. But they would sit there and talk in the house. They never walked together. Nothing was between them, just good friends.

But then another ten years were to pass and Mary was forty years old when, within a space of a year, both parents were gone. Some people said they broke their hearts over Malcolm. And of course Mary was left all alone. She never married. But she still went on her trips to the village. She brought eggs to the old people and she went to church. She went fishing. She became an old maid recluse as we would call it on the West Coast. She lived by herself.

She sold every animal on the farm, never kept one single cat. No animals, no ducks, no hens. When her parents died she gave up everything and the whole place went to grass. Her neighbours would graze their cattle or their sheep on her land. Sometimes the house would be locked up and she would be gone for weeks. No one knew where she went. Some said she was off on holiday. She had no stock to take care of. She just locked the door. Once a year she'd always for two weeks be gone. Maybe this was the reason she didn't keep any animals, because she'd go off on all these trips. Some people said she went to America, some said to Canada. But no one actually knew.

The years were to pass by. And Mary kept her own recluse way of life. An old maid. But she still kept in touch with the local minister. Mary never married, nor he never married. And his parents died. Her parents had been buried in a little cemetery with the little rough track going into the churchyard, just a muddy old road. Nice when the weather was dry, but when it was rain it got muddy.

And people had to be very careful when they walked in the old graveyard. She visited it sometimes, the grave of her parents.

Then one day when Mary was sixty years old she never appeared in the village for two days. Of course the local friend of hers, the minister, got really worried. He took a walk down to visit Mary, as all ministers do.

He went to the door and knocked. The door was open. There was no one around and he walked in. He knocked on the bedroom.

A voice said: 'Come in. Who is it?' A very weak voice.

'It's me.' Robert was his name. 'Robert.'

She says, 'Come in, Robert, I'm in bed.'

And he walked in there. By this time Mary was in her sixties, long grey hair, an old woman. She was lying in bed dressed in her nightdress.

She says, 'Robert, come sit down beside me!'

Robert came over and sat down by the bed: 'What's wrong, Mary, with you?'

'Robert, I think my time has come. Look, I think I'm going to die. But I'm going to die happy.'

'Mary, you're not going to die – we'll take care of you! Are you feeling unwell?'

'No,' she said, 'I'm not feeling unwell. I know that my time has come. And I want to pass on. I'm sixty years of age now.'

And he was fifty! Neither of the two of them were married. And of course in his own way he really loved her very much.

She says, 'Robert, would you do something for me?'

He says, 'Yes, anything, Mary!'

'Reach under my pillow.'

And he put his hand under the pillow and felt something. He brought it out. A little red book. She says, 'I won't be seeing you again. This is the last time we'll ever talk together. But I want you to do something for me.'

He says, 'Yes?'

'Well,' she says, 'look, I want you to take my little book. And I want you to read it. When I'm dead I want you to make me a promise. Everything I own is yours – I'm leaving it to the church. My parents have left me a lot of money. The land, the house – there's no one to own it but you. I'm giving it to you to sell it. I want you to give the money to the church, and share it with the old people. But I want you to promise me one thing; when I'm dead you'll put a little stone at my head.'

'Yes, Mary, of course. But you're not . . .'

'Robert, I know I'm going. I won't see you again! But I want you to give me your promise, and take my little book with you.' So he sat there and talked to her a long long time. And she says, 'All I'm asking you, Robert, is when I'm dead and buried in the little churchyard, I don't want to be buried with my parents. I want a little grave beside my parents. But I want you to find a little stone for me shaped like a heart. And I want you to put four words on that stone.'

'Of course, Mary,' he said, 'anything to please you.'

She says, 'Only four words, remember, nothing else! "To Malcolm and Mary".'

'I promise you.'

So she said, 'I think you'd better go now.'

So the minister walked off sad at heart. She had given him a letter stating that everything she owned was to go to the church – and the little red book to the minister. Two days later Mary never appeared and they found she was dead. The minister saw that everything went according to the way she wanted it to be.

Mary was laid to rest in a little grave not far from her

parents. And the minister got a little stone carved in the shape of a heart. He put it at Mary's head. The four words said TO MALCOM AND MARY. And of course the place was sold. The minister collected all the money and it went to the church.

Now . . . that graveyard was to do the villagers for many years to come. The road was never mended for another fifty years. It was just a muddy path leading into the old, old graveyard. And when people came to visit it Mary's grave was near the gate. Her grave was always well kept. There were always wild flowers on her grave. But the most important thing of all was . . . it's so sad!

Sometimes when the people walked on a Sunday after a heavy night's rain they had to walk by Mary's grave to see their relatives who were buried in the churchyard. And they saw something strange in the mud – the mark of two bare feet. The strange thing was one of the toes was missing from the footmark. People wondered where the marks had come from. No one ever knew. Only one person knew, and that was the minister. He read that book many many times. And one evening he could not keep it to himself.

So he told some of the villagers the story. He had to, before he died. And of course one of the villagers was Angus MacNeil's grandmother; before *she* died – she told Angus the strange story of 'Seal Brother'.

Glossary

aa	all
ain	own
ane	one
awa wander	stroll about
ay	always
big house	landlord's dwelling
brig	bridge
brother	dear one (male)
cannae	cannot
catcht	caught
ceilidh	house party
clabbidhus	horse mussels
clift	cliff
coo	cow
cominadae	the matter (with)
country folk	non-travellers
cowped	toppled, overturned
crack	speak; conversation
dae	do
dinnae	don't
doot	doubt
droll	strange
een	eyes
fae	from
feart	afraid
fleein	flying
frae	from
friend	relation
gae	go

gang	go a trip
garret	small upstairs room
gaun	going
gaunnae	going to
gie	give
girdle	circular iron hot-plate with hooped handle
guid	good
hae	have
haen	have had
heid	head
het	heated
hit	it (emphatic)
hoo	how
hummed and hawed	procrastinated
hus	us (emphatic)
ken	know
kinnle	kindle
knowe	knoll
laird	landlord
lir	sea
loo'd	showed affection for
mair	more
makkin	making
masel	myself
mind	remember
moich	crazy
nae	no
nane	none, any
no	not
noo	now
oxter	upper arm
ony	any
piece	slice of bread
plenty	enough of
pumps	claps (of thunder)
raik	gather; rummage
reckin jug	large clay jug for mixing
richt	right
sappy soukers	young ash branches

sellt	sold
shaifs	sheaves
shouting	talking without sense
smiddie	blacksmith's
souch	long-drawn-out sound of the wind
stane	stone
stook	set barley sheaves in a shock
stotting	walking proudly
tellt	told
the day	today
the morn	tomorrow
the noo	right now
thes	these
two-three	a few
wauken	waken
weans	children
wee bit	small amount of
wee people	the fairies
wee puckle	indefinite amount of
wee toy	very young, quite small
weel	well
wha	who
whatna	what kind of
whaur	where
wi	with
wir	our
wirsels	ourselves
worl	world
wonst	once
wrang	wrong
yer	your